Lone Star Lance

A Novel

David Studebaker

First paperback edition October 2020

Cover design and illustration by Conor McCammon
contact: cmccdesign@gmail.com

ISBN 978-0-578-78422-9

www.davidstudebaker.com

For my Tina

Author's Note

The events of this book take place in a bygone era. A simpler time. It begins in the spring of 2019; by no means an idyllic time, but compared to its older sibling, 2020, it was a true delight. So, sit back, relax and take a figurative breath of fresh, Covid-free air as we embark on Lance Ford's perilous journey to the exotic land of Dallas, Texas.

Lone Star Lance

Prologue

A short, pasty white man in a banana print novelty suit walks with trepidation down a dimly lit hotel hallway. He stops for a moment as his shifty eyes rest on a dusty painting, hanging on the blood-red wall, that reads: "DALLAS: BIG THINGS HAPPEN HERE."

A large, muscle-bound man in a suit two sizes too small stands guard at the door of Room 234 as the short man approaches and says with a wink, "You're late."

"Get inside," the stone-faced guard replies as he opens the door to a pitch-black room and moves to his left.

The short man playfully attempts to poke the guard's stomach as he passes, but before his finger can make contact, the guard grabs his wrist with predatory swiftness and begins to squeeze. "If you value your hands, you'll keep 'em away from me."

The short man moans in pain as the guard tosses him into the room and closes the door, leaving him in complete darkness.

After a few moments of silence, a sadistic voice with the sandpaper twang of a grizzled cowboy says, "Need a light, Ronald?"

A stage spotlight suddenly turns on, pointed directly at Ronald, who squints into the blinding light and wistfully replies, "Mom? Is that you?"

"It's decision time."

"Yes, hmm, so many options. I think I'll go with the grilled cheese sandwich and tomato soup. No crackers."

Ronald's joke is met with silence, broken only by the pumping of a shotgun. He nervously wipes flop sweat from his brow and mutters, "I guess I'll skip lunch."

"You know how I feel about people who waste my time."

"Of course. Down to business. Are you sure this whole plan is ethical?"

"When it comes to winning this war, ethics are irrelevant."

Ronald replies with a chuckle, "My pre-school teacher used to say the same thing. She was a hoot!"

More silence.

Ronald sighs. "Tough crowd… And what if I say no?"

"You'll be dead."

"Well… That sure clarifies things."

"No one made you swear the oath."

"But I thought they were kidding! The cloaks and the coffin and all that? I can't be the only one who found that funny."

"Get me the files and you live."

"Fine, but that's it. After that, I'm done and I'm kicking your goons out of my theater club."

The spotlight shuts off, leaving Ronald once again in complete darkness.

Chapter One

T
he towering skyscrapers of San Francisco's Financial District surround a second-story courtyard as Lance Ford, a thirty-year-old Whole Foods aficionado with soft hands, meticulously coiffed blonde hair and a swimmer's build, leads his outdoor yoga class in a shoulder stand. He takes a deep, pleasurable breath, then softly says, "Alright, let's transition to the fish pose. Remember to take it slow, Tiffany." Lance slides smoothly down from his shoulder stand and the class follows suit. After a moment on their backs, Lance and the class hoist their torsos into the fish pose. Lance lets out a deep breath and asks, "What kind of fish are we, people?"

"I'm a Steelhead Trout, swimming through the cool, fresh waters of the Russian River," replies a bearded Sociology professor.

Lance smiles. "Very nice, Paul. Let that drive your breath."

"I'm a catfish, growing stronger by the day," adds a tech entrepreneur with a job title longer than this book.

"That's how you do it, Rachel," Lance says with pride.

"I'm an unemployed fish," mumbles a sloppily dressed man in his mid-fifties.

Lance looks over with concern. "Hey now, Gerald. Keep those negative thoughts away. Employment is a state of mind, remember?"

Gerald looks unconvinced as Lance closes his eyes and returns to his breathing. Moments later, Lance's bliss is interrupted by the tap of a police baton.

"Are you the instructor?" Lance looks up into the piercing eyes of a beautiful, Latin-American police officer with a slight Texas twang in her voice.

"Yes, I am," Lance replies as he stands up and flashes an innocent smile. "What's the problem, Officer?"

"Do you have a permit to conduct business on this property?"

"Can we discuss this in private? I don't want to interrupt my class," Lance asks then adds with a whisper, "Tonya over there has very fragile chakras."

The officer rolls her eyes and nods at Lance, who turns to Sage, a white man with blonde dreadlocks. "Can you lead 'till I get back?"

Sage subtly pumps his fist while maintaining the fish pose. "I won't let you down."

Lance winks at Sage before leading the officer to a secluded walkway. Once out of sight and earshot of the class, Lance says, "Officer, I promise, the building manager is a friend of mine."

The officer pulls out her notepad and shoots him a questioning eye. "You sure about that? Because your 'friend' is the one who called in the complaint. The minimum fine is four hundred dollars."

"Four hundred?!"

"Yep," she replies without looking up from her pad.

"Is there anything I can do to change your mind?"

The officer stops writing, looks up at Lance and seductively replies, "You could start by kissing me."

Lance stares at her in disbelief. The officer takes a step towards him, wraps her arms around his waist, pulls his body up against hers and looks into his eyes. "Are you disobeying my command?"

"I wouldn't dream of it," Lance says before laying a passionate kiss on her.

"Take off your shirt," she commands as she presses him up against the wall.

"Wait, Emmy…"

"That's Officer Ford to you, Dollface," his wife replies before kissing his neck.

"What has gotten into you, Hun? I mean, I'm not complaining, but what if someone sees us?"

"I don't care. I'm handing in my badge. This job just isn't for me."

"Wait, what? You're taking the software theft defense job?" Lance asks, gently pulling away from her.

"Yep."

"What about your dream of being the next great trailblazing female detective? I was going to write a play about you."

"Well, first off, the trailblazing woman thing was your dream, I never wanted that kind of attention. And second, my dream has already come true."

"Aw, you're so sweet, but I'm not eno—"

"Not you," Emmy interrupts.

A look of hurt washes over Lance's face as Emmy sighs and says, "Well, you are a dream come true, of course, but… My other dream…"

Lance is lost. Emmy shouts with glee, "I'm pregnant!"

A wave of shock hits Lance as he stares at Emmy. However, the shock quickly turns to ecstasy as he pulls her close and holds her tight. With tears of joy filling their eyes, Lance looks down and plants a loving kiss on Emmy's lips as Sage rushes around the corner shouting, "Lance, I need you! Gerald is crying again!"

The sight of Lance kissing the police officer stops Sage in his tracks and he whispers, "Damn, that's a gangster move." He backs away and shouts at Lance, "Do your thing, Bro! Gerald's gonna be cool.

Chapter Two

Day 80 of Pregnancy

Emmy meticulously applies her makeup and puts on her favorite outfit: a shiny black blouse and tight houndstooth pants, hoping they will successfully hide the nausea-induced sleep deprivation in her eyes. She takes one last look in the mirror, makes the sign of the cross, gives her best professional smile and heads for the kitchen where her dear friend, Mr. Coffee, awaits.

After taking that first delicious gulp, instead of feeling the usual boost of adrenaline as the caffeine courses through her veins, she's met with the bubbling of her breakfast as it rises up from her stomach.

With no time to lose, Emmy slides her coffee onto the counter and sprints to the bathroom, just barely reaching the toilet before depositing her breakfast. She sits back against the wall, cold sweat dripping down her face. As the nausea subsides, she pulls herself up off the floor, looks in the mirror and fights the urge to cry at the sight. Her favorite outfit has now added a new accessory: throw up splashes.

★★★

Emmy, now wearing a dated, slightly wrinkled pantsuit, eats a dry granola bar as she sits on a hard, plastic seat in the jam-packed M train, typing on her laptop. Nearby, a bearded hipster holds a tuna fish sandwich in one hand and clips his toenails with the other. Emmy glances at him with wide-eyed astonishment and disgust as a nail clipping hits her laptop. Moments later, her train nemesis takes a large bite of his sandwich, accidentally dropping a mayonnaise lathered piece of tuna onto the floor, centimeters from Emmy's briefcase. Emmy clenches her fist and stares with disdain at the tuna as she prays under her breath, "Lord, give me the strength not to throw this man off the train."

A garbled voice comes over the loudspeaker and announces, "Next stop, Civic Center Station." Emmy's stop. She breathes a sigh of relief before closing her laptop, giving one final dirty look to the boundary-less man and standing up to exit the train.

★★★

Emmy emerges from the train station, sidestepping what she hopes is dog poop, and passes a group of men in various states of inebriation. Her heart starts to race as a member of the group begins to follow her.

"What's your name, Baby? I'll bet you look tight underneath that grandma suit."

Emmy ignores him and quickens her pace. She glances to her right and sees a man she once arrested for felony assault. The creep behind her continues to follow at an uncomfortably close distance and says, "Come on now, I know you got a voice. Every Mexican girl I've been with loves to talk."

Emmy continues to ignore her pursuer, who begins to show signs of frustration. "Baby, are you deaf? I'm tryin' to talk to you."

Emmy suddenly stops, turns around and stares him in the eyes. "Listen, I'm a former cop, a trained fighter and I'm happily married. If you know what's good for you, you'll stop following me."

"Whoa, alright, take it easy. I was just tryin' to see if you were down, but damn."

"I am definitely not 'down' and I am also not Mexican. I'm Salvadorian, you ignoramus."

"Is that near Mexico?" the man replies, genuinely confused. Emmy briefly considers educating the man on Central American geography, but that thought quickly vanishes as he continues, "Because you look hella Mexican. Are you mixed?"

"My Dad is white," Emmy says with a sigh, immediately regretting that extra bit of information as she turns to continue her walk.

"Nice, I love mixed girls. Don't you think we have a connection?"

"No, I don't. And I'm walking away. Do not follow or speak to me ever again. Got it?" Emmy marches away without waiting for a reply as the creep shakes his head in defeat and shouts, "Your loss!"

★★★

Enya's "Orinoco Flow" plays on Lance's phone alarm. He reaches out, touches the snooze button and drifts blissfully back to sleep. When he finally wakes up for good, he checks his phone and sees a text from Emmy: "Made it safe to work, my love. From now on, I'm taking Lyft." Lance responds with a sympathetic text, stretches his long arms, heads to the kitchen and boils a pot of aromatic homemade green tea.

An hour later, Lance rides with a yoga mat strapped to his back on a 1950s bicycle along the shimmering San Francisco Bay. He stops at the farmer's market in the historic Ferry Building for a vegan blueberry scone with fresh sunflower butter. After devouring his breakfast and making conversation with a sun bathing sea lion, he continues his picturesque journey in pure bliss.

The Golden Gate Bridge shines in the distance as Lance arrives at Marina Green Park and begins to prep for his yoga class. Moments later, Sage arrives looking sheepish.

"Hey Bro, just wanted to let you know this is gonna be my last class for a while."

"Why is that?" Lance replies with concern.

"I got in a fight with my dad and he's cutting off all my funds. Gonna have to go bare bones."

"Come on, Sage, you know you can still come to class. I honestly didn't even know you were paying your fees."

"Well, I wasn't, but I was meaning to, but now I can't even mean to, ya know?"

Lance laughs. "It's all good, man. You can still come. My wife works in tech so money's not really an issue."

"You're married?! What about that hot police officer?"

Emmy sits in a pretentiously decorated boardroom, surrounded by casually dressed Millennials who sit and watch with adoration as their CEO, Rick Lacey, clad in a vintage Led Zeppelin shirt, ripped jeans and Birkenstock sandals, concludes his speech. After a raucous round of applause, the group begins to file out of the room. As Emmy attempts to exit with her coworkers, Rick stops her. "Emmy... What's our motto?"

Emmy sighs then recites, "Every day is casual Friday."

"That's right. No suits necessary. We're investigating tech fraud, not running for President."

"I know, I just had some wardrobe issues this morning. The suit was all I had."

"I understand, but it's not just the suit, it's your inability to embrace the culture of my company. You haven't joined any of our office drum circles, you didn't attend Brandon's Ultimate Frisbee Championship, you continue to ignore our 'No Country Music' policy, and worst of all, you ate french fries on kale smoothie day."

"I was hungry."

"We all were. That's the point of kale smoothie day."

"Okay, maybe I haven't participated as much I could, but it's because I'm working. I've barely been here a month and my productivity rating is already the highest in the office."

"Emmy, Emmy, Emmy. There's more to this job than productivity ratings. If anything, that just further proves that you're not a team player. Instead of bumping up your own rating and solving every case, why not help Billy bump up his?"

"Okay, I'll start helping Billy with his work."

"It's too late for that. I think—"

Billy, a twenty-five-year-old Berkeley Graduate with patchy facial hair, wearing the same Led Zeppelin shirt as Rick, enters holding a green smoothie and asks, "Did you fire her yet?"

"Damn it, Billy! I was just about to do it, you idiot."

Billy looks down and replies shamefully, "I'm sorry, Rick." As his eyes begin to well with tears, he hands the green smoothie to Rick, muttering, "I made this for you."

Rick is filled with remorse as Billy storms out of the boardroom. He shouts, "Billy, wait! I didn't mean that!"

Emmy, stares in shock at Rick, who suddenly grows calm and turns back to her. "So, as I was saying…"

"I'm fired."

"Yeah. Sorry. I was going to be much smoother about it than Billy."

"He fired you?! He can't fire you!" Lance exclaims with righteous indignation as he stirs a simmering pot of marinara sauce with the care of an elderly Italian woman.

Emmy shrugs. "He's the CEO. He can do whatever he wants."

"But you have the highest productivity rating in the office!"

"That's what I said, but apparently I didn't drink enough kale smoothies."

Lance daintily tastes his sauce and says, "Well, they are extremely nutritious."

Emmy glares at Lance, who shifts back from kale to anger. "You know what, let's sue his ass. Wrongful termination."

"I was an at-will employee. I have no grounds."

Lance paces in the tiny kitchen, still holding the sauce ladle. Emmy pauses, takes a deep breath and begins her pitch. "So, I was thinking… What if we moved to Dallas?"

Lance goes bug-eyed. "Dallas?! I don't want to move to Dallas."

"Why not?"

"Um, because the weather sucks, the bugs are ginormous and everyone's a Cowboys fan. Also, your family doesn't respect me."

"My family respects you!"

"Really? Your Dad thinks I'm a pansy because I don't fish or play golf and your brother calls me 'Yoga-Boy.'"

"Oh, that was one time."

"Yeah, at our wedding reception; during his speech."

"Well, my family likes you and my parents said we could live with them and save up some money," Emmy says to Lance who stares back at her as though she just suggested they move to Folsom Prison.

Emmy rolls her eyes. "It's better than being homeless."

"That's debatable. And wait a sec, you already talked to your parents about this?"

Emmy ignores the question. "Dallas also has more jobs. Maybe you could teach Drama and use that money to fund your play."

"I write plays and I teach yoga. That's it. I don't teach actors anymore. Unless they want to learn yoga."

"So, you want to starve here?"

"We won't starve. You'll get another job."

"I don't want another job. I want my own private investigation firm."

"You can do that here. Think of all the jealous rich men in the tech world just waiting for you to stalk their wives. It's a gold mine!"

"I can do way more than just infidelity cases."

"I know. And you will, I promise. This city won't let us down."

"Wake up, Lance, it already has. The San Francisco of your youth is not the San Francisco of the present. The middle-class is gone. Pretty soon, all that will be left here are tech billionaires and homeless people. Even your parents, stalwarts of the hippie movement, abandoned-ship and moved to Miami to play Canasta."

"Yeah, well, my parents are insane. We already established that."

"Well, you know what else is insane? Our rent. We're paying four grand a month for a one-bedroom apartment. What happens when we have our child? Tell me. How do we afford that?"

Lance takes a final taste of his sauce and shakes his head at the sub-par flavor; internally pinning the Dallas conversation as the culprit for his poor performance. After a deep breath, he turns back to Emmy and says, "I don't know how, but we'll find a way, because I love this city and I am not moving to Dallas. Period."

Chapter Three

Day 98 of Pregnancy

The Downtown Dallas skyline emerges on the horizon of Interstate 30 as Lance stares in forlorn silence, gripping the steering wheel of their rented moving truck. Emmy sits next to him in the passenger seat, bobbing her head like a giddy teenager to "It's a Great Day to Be Alive," by Travis Tritt. She turns to Lance and says with a smile, "You're going to love it in Dallas, Babe. I promise."

Despite her assurance, Lance's expression is unchanged and his eyes stay locked on the road like a man driving to his death.

Lance steers the large truck into the driveway of a gorgeous, two-story Manor House and puts it in park. He looks around in awe at the sparkling University Park neighborhood and says, "Holy Toledo, I always forget how rich your parents are."

Emmy's sixty-one-year-old father, Hank, emerges from the Johnson household wearing a 'Navy Veteran' baseball cap, faded jeans and a plaid shirt that barely covers his protruding belly. Following close behind Hank is Emmy's mother, Lupita, who, despite being the same age as Hank, looks ten years younger and is dressed considerably more formal in a long, flowery dress, white cardigan sweater and low heel pumps.

Emmy excitedly hops out of the truck and leaps into Hank's arms, shouting, "Daddy! Momma!"

Lupita creates a three-way hug as Lance gingerly steps down from the truck and extends his hand. "Hi, Hank."

Hank flashes his prodigious smile and says, "Come on now, you ain't gotta call me Hank no more. Call me, King of the Castle!" Hank bellows with laughter and gives Lance a hearty pat on the back.

Lance forces an uncomfortable smile at Hank as Emmy's older brother Duke, a thirty-two-year-old former All-American UT linebacker who still wears Ed Hardy t-shirts, saunters over to join the welcome committee.

"What's up, Yoga-Boy?!" Duke boorishly says.

Lance looks down with frustration. "That's not my name."

"Ah, I'm just messin' with ya, Lancey Pants. Lighten up," Duke replies before giving Lance an aggressive pat on the back.

Emmy shoots Duke a death-glare. "Don't make me kick your ass, Duke."

"Oh, come on, Sis. I'm just playin' with the guy."

Lupita gives Duke a smack on the arm and points to the truck. "Go help Papi unload the truck, Hijo." Duke rolls his eyes and joins Hank as Lupita gives Lance a warm hug and softly says, "It's so wonderful to see you."

Hank and Lance each carry a box as they enter the palatial home, decorated with family fishing photos, crucifixes and three large, side-by-side portraits of Ronald Reagan, Troy Aikman and Our Lady of Guadalupe. Hank shoots Lance a wry smile. "What do you think, Bud? Little bigger than that postage-stamp you guys called an apartment, eh?"

Lance forces a smile. "Little bit."

Hank points to a framed picture of him and Duke holding a large fish. "Soon, you'll know that feeling."

Lance looks at the dead fish and whispers under his breath, "I already do."

Hank leads Lance down the hall towards Emmy's room. "I tell ya, your generation sure is different. I got both my kids, plus a son-in-law, still livin' in my house. Absolutely crazy."

★★★

Just three boxes remain in the truck as dusk sets in. Lance and Emmy walk down the driveway as a short, sweaty man in a bright, Italian dress shirt approaches them holding hands with his wife, a thirty-seven-year-old ex-model with a good four inches on her husband. Ronald shouts, "Howdy, Neighbors!"

Emmy perks up. "Ronald! So good to see you!" Emmy says then looks over with awe at the stunningly beautiful Judith. "Wow, Ronald, she really is a knockout. It never ceases to amaze me."

Ronald beams with pride as Judith gives a humble smile and nuzzles into him saying, "You're so sweet, thank you. I'm just trying to keep up with my handsome man."

Lance attempts to hide his confusion at this mismatched couple as Ronald smiles and gives Lance a vigorous handshake. "You must be San Francisco Lance!"

Emmy interjects, "He's Lone Star Lance now!" Lance forces a queasy smile as Emmy kisses him on the cheek and steps away to chat with Judith, leaving him alone with Ronald.

"So, Lone Star Lance, you like to shoot guns?"

"Nah, it's not really my thing."

"Too bad. I got a great gun club if you ever want to join. We hit the range every Friday night."

"Thanks, but I'm good."

Ronald lowers his voice and leans in. "It's not a gun club. We just tell our wives that. It's actually a theater club. Here's my card." Ronald hands Lance his card as Duke returns from the house. Ronald raises his voice and thickens his Texas accent. "I tell you what, you'll be hittin' them targets in no time!"

Duke grabs two of the boxes and says with a huff, "Enough chit-chattin', Lance, let's get those soft little hands on a box."

Ronald over-laughs. "Ha! Good one, Duke!"

After Duke walks back up the driveway and out of earshot, Ronald looks sheepishly at Lance and whispers, "Sorry about that."

Lance asks with sudden curiosity, "Is Duke in the theater club?"

Ronald laughs and shakes his head. "Absolutely not."

"Good to know. Either way though, I don't think I'm interested."

"Please, just consider it. You have my card."

Ronald gives Lance a cheesy smile then walks over to Judith and Emmy. Lance looks down at Ronald's card which reads: "RONALD KOZLOWSKI – PROFESSIONAL BULLSHITTER" with no contact information. Lance sighs and mutters under his breath, "Where am I?"

★★★

The ornate living room fireplace is aglow as an exhausted Emmy and Lance cuddle up on the plush sectional couch. Hank and Duke sit in their respective La-Z-Boys watching a Texas Rangers game as Lupita enters carrying a tray of hot cocoa and looks at Emmy with concern. "You sure you don't want a cup?"

Emmy shakes her head. "I'm sure. The taste of chocolate suddenly makes me nauseous."

Lupita looks at her daughter with knowing sympathy and says, "It will all be worth it when your little one arrives, but, oh! Those pregnancy stomach aches."

"That's what happens when you get knocked up. Shoulda used protection, Sis!" Duke interjects with a loud laugh, looking around like a bad stand-up comedian realizing his joke has bombed.

Lupita's ever faithful, old school Catholic matriarch blood begins to boil with righteous anger as she grabs Duke's hot cocoa off the side table, storms out of the room and pours it down the kitchen sink. Duke yells after her, "Mom! That's my cocoa!"

"Hey, Duke, how are you and Darlene doing?" Emmy asks, already knowing the answer.

"None of your business," Duke replies defensively.

Hank laughs. "That's a bit of a sore subject, Emmy."

Emmy feigns surprise. "Really? What happened?"

Duke grips the leather arms of his chair and stares at the TV. "I don't wanna talk about it."

Hank looks over at Lance and says with a grunt, "She dumped his ass."

"No, she just said if I didn't propose by the end of the year she was leaving. I didn't want to propose, so she left."

Lance gives a tired nod and sips his cocoa; thankful the conversation has nothing to do with him.

Emmy continues to probe. "Why didn't you propose?"

"I just wasn't ready to settle down, okay? I don't play that ultimatum game."

"Duke, you're thirty-two. You guys were living together for five years. You're such a man-child."

Duke looks to Hank for support. "Really, Dad? I make a harmless joke and Mom takes my cocoa. Emmy calls me a man-child and nothing...?"

Lance whispers to Emmy, "Is he serious?" Emmy stifles a laugh and nods.

"Hey, I liked Darlene and I need you to carry on the Johnson family name, so don't look at me, Big Fella," Hank replies, then turns his attention back to the game.

Duke angrily stands up, opens the door to the vintage liquor cabinet and grabs a bottle of whiskey before storming away while muttering various expletives.

"This cocoa is fantastic," Lance says to no one in particular.

★★★

The full weight of their exhausting move hits Emmy and Lance as they collapse into bed. Emmy snuggles her pillow, closes her eyes and whispers, "Sleep tight, my love."

Lance seals his organic facial moisturizer, the final step in a five-part night-time skin regimen, before placing it on the bedside stand, turning out his light and attempting to get comfortable on the squeaky double bed with Emmy fast asleep next to him. Just as Lance begins to drift off, thunderous snoring roars from the adjacent living room. He attempts to ignore it, but the volume of the snoring continues to build. He puts a pillow over his head, but the snoring forces its way through the cotton into his ears. He takes the pillow off of his head and stares wide-eyed at the ceiling before getting out of bed to investigate the source of the snoring.

Lance tiptoes into the living room and finds Duke, passed out on the couch, snoring in a drunken stupor. He approaches the couch and tries to determine if he can shift Duke on his side without waking him up. Lance takes a deep breath, leans over and lifts Duke's thick arm without noticing the TV remote still in his hand, which falls from his limp hand and crashes onto the hardwood floor. Lance freezes in terror.

Duke's snoring stops, but his eyes stay closed in slumber. Before Lance can sneak away, Duke sleepily mumbles, "Come here, Darlene," and pulls Lance in to cuddle. Lance desperately tries to silently wriggle free, but cannot escape, then freezes as Lupita pads down the stairs, passes through the dark living room and into the kitchen. Moments later, Lupita returns with a glass of milk and whispers, "Glad to see you boys are getting along," then heads back upstairs.

After a few moments of horrified silence, Lance makes another attempt to break free, but Duke's grip only tightens as Emmy enters the living room, looks at the scene in sleepy confusion and whispers, "Lance, what are you doing?"

Lance whispers back, "I'm trying to stop his snoring!"

"By cuddling with him?"

"Obviously, this did not go as planned."

Emmy walks over to Duke and shakes his arm. "Wake up, ya big bear."

Lance manages to break free from Duke's grasp and hops off the couch as the snoring lug mumbles, "Huh? What?"

"You're snoring. Roll over," Emmy impatiently informs him.

Duke moans and turns onto his stomach, eyes still closed. Emmy gives Lance a sideways glance and heads back into the bedroom. He takes a deep breath and starts to follow her when Duke sleepily whispers, "Thanks for the cuddles, Lance."

Lance stops in his tracks, eyes wide with fear at the thought of Duke being conscious during the ordeal. After a few moments of silence, he continues his journey back to the bedroom where he finds Emmy already asleep. The exhausted man climbs into bed and attempts to calm down with deep, mindful breaths. Just as he begins to drift off to sleep, the silence is broken yet again by Duke's snoring.

"He's going to be the death of me," Lance whispers to himself, fully in the throes of self-pity.

Chapter Four

Day 99 of Pregnancy

Emmy sits in bed, typing swiftly on her laptop in an excited rush to fill out her forms with the Texas Private Security Bureau and get her investigation agency up and running. Lance wakes up next to her in a tangle of blankets with a sober hangover. Emmy gives Lance a kiss good-morning as he rolls off the bed and rifles through one of several moving boxes on the ground. After some struggle, Lance pulls out a stick of incense, lights it and holds it under his nose.

"Rough night?" Emmy asks, simultaneously amused and sympathetic.

"I don't want to talk about it."

"Can I tell you something cool? I just filed my paperwork. Once they process it, I will officially be a licensed Private Investigator in the state of Texas!"

"Way to go, Hun!" Lance replies with all the enthusiasm he can muster and walks over to give her a kiss. As he pulls away, Emmy looks back at him with a pained expression on her face.

"Is my breath that bad?"

"No," she replies, brushing him aside and rushing out of the room saying, "the incense!"

Lance guiltily snuffs out the incense as the sound of Emmy's puke splattering into the toilet echoes from the adjacent bathroom.

★★★

A tall, shapely woman in a skin-tight black dress and red-bottom heels, catwalks down the dimly lit, red hotel hallway, stopping to address the muscle-bound guard at room 234. "He still has you on door-duty, Chet? No promotion?"

Chet smirks. "I'm the only one he trusts."

"Smart man," she replies, running her finger seductively along his washboard stomach.

"Aren't you married?"

"It's a job, not a marriage."

Chet laughs. "Well, when you finish the job, we can talk."

"You're so traditional. I love it."

Chet opens the door and steps to the side. "Let's not keep him waiting."

She gives his crotch a love-tap and heads inside the room. Chet closes the door, leaving her in total darkness. A spotlight turns on, flooding her eyes with blinding light.

"Is that really necessary?" she asks, utterly unimpressed by the theatrics.

"Desperate times, Judith. Desperate times…"

"But I already know who you are. What's the point?"

The cowboy cackles. "I'm goin' to let you in on a little secret. I ain't Big Jim. I was watchin' every one of your meetings with him over the years, but I'm just a shadow to you."

Judith does her best to act as though she already knew that information. After a long pause, the cowboy continues, "I'm worried about Ronald."

"Well, you shouldn't be. He's fully on board with the mission."

"He better. Otherwise, his blood will be on your hands. Literally."

"I'm aware of the deal."

"Good. Have you found a target, yet?"

"Yes. Actually, Ronald found one for me."

"Ronald? But he's not supposed to know."

"That's the best part. Ronald has no idea. And amazingly, he's still under the impression that I think he's actually in a gun club, which would be insulting if he wasn't such a profoundly stupid man. But all the boys you planted in that club might actually have to do some acting because he wants the target to help them put on a play."

The cowboy laughs joylessly. "Beautiful. What's the dead man's name?"

"Lance Ford."

★★★

Lance, Emmy, Lupita, Hank and Duke sit at a round table in the upscale Royal Oaks Country Club restaurant. An elegant waiter sets down a tray filled with gargantuan plates of salad. Lance stares wide-eyed at the plates. "That's the small salad?"

The waiter smoothly replies, "Yes, sir."

"This is more salad than I eat in a month. And I eat a lot of salad," Lance says as he grabs the wrong fork and takes a stab at the mountain of lettuce in front of him. "Does the dressing come in a bathtub?"

Lupita deftly changes the subject. "So, Lance, have you written any new plays lately?"

"I'm actually just finishing my latest. It's a modern adaptation of G.K. Chesterton's novel, *Napoleon of Notting Hill*. It's all about the fight to maintain passion and vibrancy in a bland, cold world."

Duke snorts. "Sounds boring."

Emmy punches Duke in the arm. Duke winces as Lupita steps in. "Esmerelda, we are in public."

"Mom, can you please call me, Emmy? You know I hate Esmerelda."

"But it's a beautiful name, Hija!" Lupita replies. She turns to Lance and says, "We agreed that Hank would name our boys and I would name our girls."

Duke gulps down a shot of whiskey and puts his arm around Lance. "That's why I got the white name and she got the Latin name."

"So, I've been wondering, how much money do you make writin' those plays, Lance?" Hank asks with a folksy method of questioning honed over decades as a trial lawyer.

Lance fights through a mouthful of lettuce before answering, "Not much. I actually lost money on my last production."

Emmy feels the judgment mounting and interjects, "It was fantastic though, and he got a great review in the San Francisco Chronicle. It just takes time to get established, but down the road there could be some good money to be made, right, Honey?"

"Yeah, maybe."

Hank lets out a patronizing chuckle. "So, I take it you'll be living with us for a while, then."

Lance looks down at his salad, determined more than ever to find a way out of that house. "No, I'm planning on getting a high school teaching job as soon as possible."

Emmy looks at Lance with surprised confusion. "You are?"

"Yeah. We talked about that, Babe."

"But you said that—"

"I said that I love teaching drama and it'll allow you to get your private investigation firm off the ground."

Lupita smiles. "That's wonderful, Lance. Teaching is a very honorable profession. Hank, you should call Principal Dwyer, see if he's still hiring."

Hank looks across the restaurant and stands up. "Yeah, let's go talk to him, Lance."

Lance instantly regrets his lie as the color retreats from his face. "He's here?"

"He's always here. His wife's a terrible cook," Hank says with a knowing smile.

Lupita puts her hand on Hank's arm. "We're in the middle of dinner. It can wait."

"We'll be quick," Hank says, then summons Lance, who looks like a deer in headlights as he stands up and follows Hank across the restaurant.

Principal Dwyer wears an impeccably tailored suit over his tall, thin frame as he cuts his steak with unsettling precision and takes a robotic bite. Across the table sits his wife, who wears the same style of pantsuit that Emmy was fired in and stares icily out the window as Hank approaches and gives Principal Dwyer a friendly pat on the back.

"Hello, Hank, to what do I owe this meal interruption?"

"Dwyer, this is Lance, my son-in-law. He's a drama teacher. You should hire him."

Lance offers Dwyer an apologetic smile as the principal focuses his icy gaze on him. "And why is that?"

"Well, he was one of San Francisco's top playwrights and he is an absolutely incredible teacher. He could teach your dog to speak French."

Lance shakes his perspiring head. "No, that's really—"

Hank silences Lance with a stern look. Lance gives a thumbs-up and says, "Oui!"

"And get this, he can name every single Shakespeare play ever written," Hank says, motioning for Lance to start naming titles.

"Uh, yeah, *Romeo and Juliet, Comedy of Errors, Hamlet, A Midsummer Night's Dream, Othello, Merchant of Venice*—"

"Alright, alright," Dwyer interrupts. "I do happen to have a position available. Here's my card. Swing by my office tomorrow and don't interrupt my dinner ever again."

Hank smiles triumphantly. "You're a good man, Dwyer."

Lance whispers to Hank as they head back to their table, "That was incredible. Thanks, Hank!"

"You're welcome. Just don't screw this up. Dwyer's a loose cannon and has a lot of pull here with tee times. If you piss him off, I'll be golfin' at noon in the summer and four A.M. in the winter."

"Got it. Totally. I'll be careful."

★★★

As the family embarks on another nightly fireside hot cocoa ritual, Emmy snuggles into Lance and looks up at him with admiration, "I'm so happy for you, Hun."

Lance deflects, "I owe it all to Hank. His lawyerly skills were on full display."

Hank pours a shooter of whiskey into his cup of hot chocolate and says with folksy pride, "It's what I do."

Duke pours two shooters of whiskey into his cup and snorts. "If you ask me, that job sounds horrible. Gotta teach those little weirdos how to say, 'To be or not to be.' I'll stick to personal training, thank you very much."

Before Emmy can lob an insult at Duke, the front door opens and Ronald enters, startling Lance and no one else.

"Good evenin' y'all!" Ronald says with a smile and a wave.

Hank looks over at Ronald and bellows, "Hiya, Ronald!" then turns his attention back to the television.

Lance, still unnerved, whispers to Emmy, "He just walks in? No knock?"

Emmy whispers back, "Of course. He's our neighbor."

"So? One of our neighbors in San Francisco was a sex offender."

"Yeah, one of the many reasons why we're in Dallas."

"Like you don't have sex offenders in Dallas," an offended Lance sarcastically replies.

"Well, at least they're not living in the same building as us," Emmy says before turning away from Lance, effectively ending the whispered bickering as Ronald walks over to Lupita and takes a deep, pleasurable breath. "Smells like someone made her famous hot cocoa."

Lupita smiles, flattered. "You want a mug?"

"I'd love one, thank you!" Ronald says as Lupita stands up and heads for the kitchen.

Lance whispers to Emmy, "And he's getting cocoa?!"

"Have a seat, Ron," Hank says without looking away from the television.

Ronald declines, "Actually, I was wondering if I could borrow Lance for a quick chat."

Lance, wishing he had an invisibility cloak, asks with suspicion, "Me? Why?"

"It's a bit of a private matter. Mind if we take a stroll?"

Lance looks to Emmy hoping she'll provide an excuse. Nothing. Lupita returns and hands Ronald a mug.

"Thank you, kindly," he says to Lupita, then ushers Lance out the door.

Emmy looks at the closed door and gives Lupita a wry smile. "Lance is already making friends."

Outside, Lance and Ronald stroll leisurely along the empty sidewalk. After some awkward silence, Ronald sighs and turns to Lance. "I have to apologize."

Lance looks confused. "Why?"

"When we met, I knew you were a playwright, but I had no idea I was in the midst of a professional! You're downright famous!"

Lance chuckles. "Yeah, so famous that no one in San Francisco would fund my last play."

"Well, I google'd you and it said you were voted San Francisco's favorite playwright."

"Yeah, that was seven years ago. And the competition wasn't exactly stiff. I guarantee I am no longer San Francisco's favorite playwright."

"Well, this ain't San Francisco."

"Oh, I know," Lance replies with a pained sigh.

Ronald stares up at the sky wistfully. "I have so much respect for artists. I really envy you."

"You envy me? I'm dead broke and I live with my in-laws."

"You're an inspiration. Now, listen, I have a proposition. The guys in the 'gun club,' myself included, have been feeling guilty about hiding our love of theater from our wives and we want to come out to them as aspiring actors, but we don't know how."

"Why didn't you just tell them in the first place?"

"You've seen my wife. She's way out of my league. We're not even in the same sport, but she married me because I'm a tough, confident provider." Lance looks with skepticism at Ronald's assertion of toughness as the odd man continues, "I thought, if she found out I can cry on command, she'd lose respect for me. Suddenly, her boss, Big Jim, starts looking more and more enticing. Before I know it, she's gone and I'm left with two cats and a mortgage."

"Damn that Big Jim," Lance says facetiously.

Ronald looks worried. "You know him?"

Lance shakes his head. "Get to the point."

"The point. Yes. Well, as I read about you, I had an epiphany. We have money. You have expertise. So, what if we pooled our resources together and produced one of your plays? It would be great! You could direct it, we could star in it and on opening night we could come out to our wives!"

"Weird, but go on..."

"I can see it now: 'Famous San Francisco playwright Lance Ford brings his critically acclaimed play to Dallas!'" Ronald says as Lance laughs with feigned humility.

"So, you're in?" Ronald presses.

"No."

"Why not?"

"My plays require polished, experienced actors. Not, uh... You. Sorry."

"Please, just come to our next meeting. We have some incredible audition monologues."

"I don't know. I have a lot going on right now."

"I'll pay you for your time."

"How much?"

"Four hundred."

Lance looks shocked at the high price. "Four hundred?"

Ronald misinterprets the look from Lance. "Okay, fine. Five hundred."

"You want to pay me five hundred bucks to watch some monologues?"

"Is that not enough?"

"No, that's... I'm in."

Ronald pumps his fist. "Yes! Meeting is Friday night at eight," Ronald pauses, then adds, "oh, and you can't tell anyone; for now. As far as they know, it's still a gun club."

Lance looks uneasy. "I don't like that."

Ronald counters, "Six hundred dollars."

Lance's determination to build up his finances and get his own home trumps his discomfort with the secrecy. "My lips are sealed."

Chapter Five

Day 100 of Pregnancy

E mmy sits on the bed doing her usual morning laptop work as Lance rummages through their moving boxes with an expression of consternation. She looks over at her husband suspiciously. "I still can't believe you're really joining a gun club."

"I'm not joining. I'm just… Checking it out."

"What happened to America needing to ban all guns? Isn't that what you always say?"

"I'm evolving."

Emmy's laptop dings. She clicks on the track-pad, reads her new e-mail and cheers. "My license is officially active!"

Lance rushes over and gives her a congratulatory kiss, then returns to searching through the boxes. Emmy asks, "What're you looking for?"

"My face lotion. I can't find it."

"Did you check the bathroom?"

"Yeah, twice. If I don't have that lotion, my skin is going to be super dry which will distract me during the entire interview and ruin my chances."

"You're going to be fine, Honey. Principal Dwyer will love you no matter what."

Lance dumps an entire box on the floor. "Tell that to Hank."

"Oh, Dad's just being dramatic. He is a very nice man and you will nail the interview."

"I better. We need to get out of this house."

Duke bursts into the bedroom wearing nothing but a towel. "Hey, Yoga-Boy! I used the rest of your face lotion. Hope that's okay. I had some real bad chafing down in the man-parts and it was the only thing I could reach from the toilet. Thanks, Bro!"

Duke jogs out of the room and upstairs, leaving a disgusted Lance staring in horrified silence. Emmy puts down her laptop to comfort Lance, "I'll make sure he buys you a new one."

Before Lance can respond, a booming voice echoes from the living room, "Hello?! Anyone home?!"

Lance shoots Emmy a worried look. "Are your parents home?"

"No, they left for the lake already," Emmy calmly replies.

Lance rushes out of the bedroom to investigate. He swiftly tip-toes down the hallway, peaks around the corner and sees a man in his seventies wearing a cowboy hat, plaid shirt and a pistol strapped to his belt, all while holding a fruit basket.

Lance shouts, "He has a gun! And fruit?"

The man offers him a friendly smile. "You must be Lance. I'm Art."

Lance presses, "How did you get in here?"

"I walked in. No one locks their doors 'round here, Lance."

"How do you know my name?"

"Relax, Son. I live next door. We met at your wedding. Also, that Ronald character works for me and gives me neighborhood updates whether I want 'em or not, so I know a lot about you. Speakin' of which, I heard you're joinin' his little gun club."

"What? He said that? No, I am going to one meeting as a favor. I am not joining the gun club."

"I'm with ya, Partner. I don't need a club to enjoy my guns, either. I do that mighty fine on my own."

Emmy enters the living room and smiles. "Arty! I knew that was you."

"Howdy, Gorgeous! I brought y'all a welcome gift," Art says and hands Emmy the fruit basket.

"Aw, that's so sweet, thank you. I hope Lance didn't scare you," Emmy replies, laughing with Art a little too hard at the joke. Realizing Lance's feelings are hurt, she changes the subject. "You know, Hun, you're in the midst of a celebrity."

Art looks around the room incredulously. "Is there someone else here I don't know about?"

"He's being modest. Art is the founder and CEO of Altitude Airlines."

"Are you serious? That's my favorite airline!" Lance says, suddenly in fan-boy mode.

"Well, thank you for your business," Art replies, then reaches into his pocket and hands Lance a pin with wings and the Altitude Airlines logo. "Here you go, Partner. Hope it brings you good luck at your interview today."

"Good God, you know about my interview, too?"

"Yes indeed. And I don't envy you. That Dwyer is a real piss-ant. Got a hair-trigger temper."

"Well, that's comforting," Lance remarks sarcastically before nervously touching his face and saying with a groan, "I can already feel my face getting flaky."

Art looks on with confusion as Lance gives him a defeated salute and heads back to the bedroom. He turns to Emmy and says with a kind-hearted chuckle, "They definitely make 'em different in San Francisco."

"He's a little stressed."

"I understand," Art replies and lowers his voice. "Emmy, could I ask you for a favor?"

"Of course, what's up?"

"Well, first off, congratulations on gettin' that license."

Emmy smiles. "Dad already told you?"

"He did." Art's demeanor suddenly looks pained as he says, "He also told me about what happened at that garbage tech company. Now, listen, I happen to have some friends who are clients of that dirt-bag CEO and unless you say otherwise, I'm goin' to put in a few calls and suggest they take their business elsewhere. No one messes with my goddaughter and gets away with it."

Emmy laughs. "Aw, you're so sweet, Arty, but no, please don't. Rick firing me was an absolute blessing. I wouldn't be home without it and I couldn't be happier."

"Ol' Lance there looks like he could be a little happier."

Emmy sighs. "Yeah, he's adjusting. So, what's the favor?"

"Right, well, it's about my son-in-law, Jack."

"Yeah, I know Jack, is everything okay?"

"Hard to say, you see, he's been actin' a little funny lately. My little Madison thinks he's cheatin' on her, but my gut tells me somethin' else is goin' on, I just can't put my finger on it. You think you could look into it for me?"

"Of course. And you're sure you have no ideas?"

"Honestly, I don't. And normally I don't like to trifle in another man's marriage, even if he is married to my daughter, but the thing is, I'm retirin' at the end of the year and some folks on the board are lookin' for any excuse to sell the company. Now, Jack has been a superstar for us and we have enough allies on the board that we should be able to make him CEO and keep the company. I just need to know that Altitude is goin' to be in good hands. I can't let our sixty thousand employees be put at the mercy of some soul-less, profit-squeezin' multi-national corporation, but I also need to know that Jack is the man I think he is."

"Totally understand. I'm on it."

Art smiles with solemn gratitude. "Thank you. Now, I'm goin' to have to pay you in cash, though. No one at the company can know about this."

"You don't have to pay me."

"Listen here, if I can pay that buffoon Ronald to do whatever the hell it is he does at my company, you bet your ass I'm goin' to pay a top quality private eye what she's worth."

"Well, it's an honor to work for you," Emmy says as she hugs Art. Her demeanor grows somber as she asks, "How are you holding up?"

"I'm survivin.' Ain't a day goes by that I don't miss my Wynona, but I know she's in Heaven and I feel her watchin' me every day."

"She is. And I pray for you and Madison every day."

"Thank you, my dear. Madison is just like her mom, so I still have a piece of Wy on Earth. But enough of the weepy stuff. Go help your boy."

Emmy gives Art a kiss on the cheek before parting.

Back in the bedroom, Lance lies on the floor in a difficult yoga pose, attempting to calm his nerves. Emmy rushes in smiling from ear to ear. "I got my first client!"

"That's amazing. Who?" Lance replies with his eyes still closed, mid-exhale.

"Altitude Airlines!"

Lance opens his eyes, deliberately stands up from his pose, gives Emmy a congratulatory hug and asks, "What're you looking into?"

Emmy hems, "I shouldn't talk about it."

"Come on, I'm your husband."

"Literally, you cannot tell a soul," she says with a sigh. "Not even that I'm working for Art or Altitude."

Lance nods as Emmy lowers her voice and continues, "He wants me to tail his son-in-law. See if he's up to anything shady."

"Absolutely not."

"What?"

"I thought you were just going to do white collar stuff until the baby is born. What if this guy notices you watching him and assaults you?"

"You really think I'm that bad of a detective? Plus, I know him, he's not the violent type."

"That's what they always say about mass murderers. 'Oh, he was the nicest man. We had no idea!'"

"You're being ridiculous."

"I am protecting our unborn child."

"Didn't you want to make a bunch of money so we can get our own place?"

"Not at the expense of your safety. Plus, how much is really paying you?"

"Two hundred dollars an hour with no maximum."

Lance stares at her in disbelief, realizing he's lost all leverage. "Well… That's… Wow. Okay, um I'll make you a deal, if you do any stakeouts after sundown, I come with you."

"I can protect myself, Hun. And wouldn't daytime be more dangerous for them to see me? Either way though, I'll be fine and I still have my open-carry permit so I'll be armed."

"Yeah, you and everyone else in this town. I feel like I'm in the Wild West. So, I'm coming with you whether you like it or not. And just look at it this way, you're doing your job and I'm baby-sitting our child."

Emmy relents. "Fine, you can come, but when we're in the field and I tell you to do something, you do it. No questions."

"Deal."

"Art said Jack usually disappears Friday after work, so tomorrow we'll go over all the stakeout guidelines so that you'll be up to speed by the evening."

Lance winces. "Ahh, tomorrow night's actually no good for me. I have that stupid gun club meeting."

"Just tell Ronald you'll go another time."

"I can't do that. He's paying me."

Now it's Emmy's turn to stare at Lance in fiduciary disbelief. "He's paying you? To go to his gun club?"

Lance searches for a way to explain without lying. "Yeah, apparently he thinks I was some kind of celebrity in San Francisco and when I declined his offer to join the club, he said he'd pay me to show up."

"How much?"

"Six hundred dollars."

Emmy laughs. "You're kidding."

"Nope."

"Well, then you better start polishing up your guns."

★★★

Principal Dwyer sits in a cushy executive chair at his large, ornate desk; the only frivolous items in his sparsely decorated office. With the distinctly joyless eyes of a hardened administrator, he reviews a stack of paperwork, occasionally making notes as Lance opens the door and enters with caution.

For a few tense moments, Principal Dwyer keeps his eyes on the paperwork, ignoring Lance, who hesitates, then says, "Howdy."

Dwyer looks up from his paperwork and eyes his prey. "Howdy? How often do you say, 'howdy?'"

"Uh, not very often?" Lance replies, suddenly stripped of all confidence.

"Don't say 'howdy.' Have a seat."

Lance sits down in a tiny plastic chair and looks up at Dwyer, who looms high in his throne and asks, "So, you're from San Francisco?

"Born and raised."

"Interesting. What do you think of Dallas?"

Lance hesitates. "I, I like it."

Dwyer leans forward. "Don't lie to me."

"I'm not lying," Lance replies, attempting to look innocent.

"Do I frighten you?"

"No."

"Another lie. Tell me the truth."

"Okay, maybe a little?"

"Thank you," Dwyer says as he leans back in his chair and relaxes his expression. "You know, many moons ago, I got my master's degree at USF."

"Really?" Lance replies, feigning interest.

"Some of the best times of my life were spent in San Francisco," Dwyer says wistfully and chuckles. "Don't tell Hank, but I was actually a bit of a hippie. We'd go down to City Hall, smoke some dope and protest the war. Do you smoke?"

Lance hesitates, Dwyer waves him off and says, "Don't answer that." They share a chuckle as Dwyer takes a sip from his tiny glass of orange juice and asks, "Are you a sports fan?"

"Yes, sir. Giants, Niners and Warriors for life."

"Ahh, well I won't hold that against you."

Lance gives a gratuitous fake laugh and asks, "What about you?"

"Cowboys, Mavs, Longhorns and Rangers."

"Rangers, eh? Sorry about that 2010 World Series."

"No, you're not."

They laugh in unison. Lance continues his ribbing of Texas sports. "And sorry about the Cowboys."

Dwyer's expression suddenly darkens. "What's wrong with the Cowboys?"

Drunk with confidence, Lance continues, oblivious to Dwyer's sudden exit from the joking exchange, "Where to begin? They're the most overrated, over-hyped franchise in sports."

"Well, I wouldn't say that," Dwyer replies, hiding his growing rage.

"Come on, Dak Prescott? Are you kidding me? How many times has that guy choked? Only one who was a bigger choker than Dak was Romo."

Dwyer seethes. "Tony Romo is a close, personal friend of mine."

"Well, then I hope you know the Heimlich maneuver."

Principal Dwyer stands up in a fit of rage and warns, "Watch your mouth, Pinhead."

Lance leans back in surprise, attempting to diffuse the situation. "Whoa, take it easy, I thought we were just joking around."

"Tony is not a joke."

Lance wants to make one last retort, but holds it in and says, "I'm sorry."

Dwyer stares into Lance's eyes. "That wasn't what you wanted to say."

Lance attempts to look innocent. "Seriously, I'm sorry."

Dwyer slams his hand on the desk and shouts, "Tell me what you were going to say."

"Come on, we're both San Francisco brothers, let's just move on, shall we? Nothing to get angry about."

"Tell me. Now."

Lance exhales in defeat. "Okay, when you said Tony is not a joke, I was going to say, and again, I would have been totally kidding, but I wanted to say, 'his playoff record was a joke.'"

Dwyer stares stone-faced at Lance and allows an uncomfortably long silence to fall on the room before pointing to the door and saying, "Get out of my office."

★★★

Lance lies on the living room floor looking defeated. Emmy sits next to him, legs crossed, sympathetically stroking his hair. "Can I make you a blueberry scone?" she softly asks.

Lance forlornly shakes his head. "I don't deserve a scone." The sound of the garage door vibrating through the house causes Lance to moan. "Oh God, your dad's home. I'm a dead man."

Emmy attempts to assuage him. "Oh, it's no big deal, he was just being dramatic about the golf stuff."

Hank enters the living room, his face the color of red due to both frustration and a long, sunny day at the lake. He looks at his son-in-law and says, "Jesus Lance, what in the blue hell happened in that interview today?! Dwyer's goin' ballistic and I'm doin' my best to stay calm, but it ain't easy."

Lance stands up to face the music as Lupita, following close behind Hank, slaps her husband's arm and points at him with a reproachful finger. "Hank, for the last time, do not use El Señor's name in vain."

Hank looks guiltily at Lupita. "I'm sorry, Honey."

Lupita points at the Crucifix on the wall. "Apologize to Him."

Hank turns to the wall and grumbles like a fifth grader in detention, "I'm sorry, Jesus."

A somber Lupita adds, "Padre, perdónalo porque no sabe lo que hace," then turns to Hank. "And be nice to your son-in-law."

Hank forces a smile and softly asks Lance, "I won't be mad, just tell me what happened so I can deal with Dwyer accordingly."

"It was so crazy, everything was going well, we were hitting it off and then we started talking sports, I made a harmless little joke about Tony Romo and he went ballistic. I think the guy is really unstable."

Hank sighs. "Damn. I should've warned you. Dwyer's obsessed with Tony Romo. Duke made a joke about Romo once and Dwyer threw a beer at him."

"What?! That's insane. Are they really friends?"

"I don't think so. Far as I know, they met for three minutes at a charity golf tournament and Dwyer's been obsessed with him ever since. The man hasn't played a down of football in years, but I guess Dwyer's still as sensitive about him as ever. Regardless, we need to fix this."

Lance nods. "Whatever you need me to do, I'll do."

"You're goin' to regret that ma boy," Hank says with a laugh, then notices his wife and daughter shooting him warning glares. "Jokes. It's all jokes. I'll take care of everything."

Chapter Six

Day 101 of Pregnancy

Lance sits at the kitchen table eating unsweetened brown rice puff cereal with flaxseed milk and fresh strawberries. He checks the temperature on his mug of tropical green tea, feels it's just right, takes a therapeutic smell and sip, then whispers to himself, "What would I do without Whole Foods?"

Emmy sits across the table from Lance, eyes locked on her laptop screen. She reaches for a saltine cracker without looking up, takes a bite and continues to work. Lance looks at her meager meal with concern and says, "You sure that's enough food, Babe?"

Emmy replies without looking up, "It's the only thing I can keep down right now."

"Can I at least get you some water?"

"Water's been making me nauseous lately," Emmy says, still focused on her work.

"You can't have water now? What's next? Air?"

Lance shrugs, turning his attention back to his breakfast. Moments later, the tranquility is shattered by Hank who walks into the kitchen carrying a dusty bag of golf clubs and proclaims, "Dwyer's agreed not to screw me!"

"Awesome," Lance replies, relieved, then sees Hank set down the dusty golf clubs next to him, which sends waves of anxiety flowing through his body.

"I told him what a terrible golfer you are and he said if you play a round of eighteen with us tomorrow morning, I can keep my regular tee times."

"I have to golf with that lunatic?"

"Yes. And you have to lose. Which shouldn't be too hard for you…"

Emmy interjects, "Dad, isn't this a little much?"

"Let's just call it rent," Hank says with a wink as he grabs a bagel and heads out of the kitchen.

Lance stares mournfully at the dusty golf clubs while Emmy attempts to change the subject. "You know, I had an idea, a girlfriend of mine from high school just opened up a yoga studio downtown, I'm sure she could use an amazing instructor like you on the team."

Lance takes a moment to think about it then shakes his head. "I think I'm done teaching yoga. I'm realizing, without the ocean breeze, being a yoga instructor just doesn't feel right. I actually had a different idea I wanted to run by you… What if you hired me to be your deputy? I know I'll be there to babysit at night, but what if I really dig in and help you with your work during the day? By the time you're too pregnant to go out in the field, I'll be experienced enough to take over! I'll be the Robin to your Batwoman. The Captain America to your Captain Marvel. The white guy whose name I can't remember in Beverly Hills Cop to your Eddie Murphy."

Emmy laughs like a kindergarten teacher whose student just pledged to build a spaceship. "You sure you're up for that?"

"So sure. Don't forget, in college I wrote a one-act play about a private detective and the school paper hailed it for its authenticity," Lance smiles with pride, half-joking, half-serious.

"Those are pretty rock-solid credentials."

"Thank you. So, let's get started, shall we?"

"Okay, while you were sleeping, I printed out the supporting documents and internal files from Art for the Altitude case file. It's just a start, but if you want to be a full partner this is what you'll have to dig into on a regular basis."

Emmy pulls a large cardboard box from under the kitchen table, takes off the cover and reveals hundreds of pages of documents. She grabs a handful of papers from the top and slides them across the table to Lance as he stares at the stack with wide-eyed trepidation. Emmy smiles and asks, "What do you say, Captain America?"

Lance slowly looks up from the stack. "I say that is an incredible waste of paper and it better have been made from post-consumer waste. Also, I'm thinking maybe we stick with our original agreement."

Emmy nods in triumph. "Deal."

★★★

Ronald stares back at his reflection in the full-length mirror hanging on the door of his expansive master bedroom walk-in closet. Clad in a cashmere black mock turtleneck, he gives his best brooding, emotional expression, holds it for a few seconds then says, "And Scene!"

He looks around the room at an imaginary film crew and sighs with flattery. "Oh, thank you, Mr. Spielberg, I don't know if it was the perfect take, but if it's good enough for you, it's good enough for me."

Ronald's fantasy is interrupted by the sound of Judith entering the house. He swiftly takes off the turtleneck, throws it at the bottom of his open rifle bag, grabs a white t-shirt and Dickies jacket from the closet and puts on his shooting attire.

Judith enters the room wearing a tight exercise outfit and puts on her signature manipulative charm. "How was work, Handsome?"

"Exhausting, I built three planes all by myself. Just turnin' those screwdrivers, righty tighty, lefty loosey."

Judith fake laughs. "Did Art tell you how the board meeting went?"

"Yeah, he said they're still weighing their options, but it looks like he has the votes for Jack to climb the ol' bean stock and take over. Which, I know we're supposed to hate the guy and all, but ever since he joined the gun club, I've seen a new side to him. He's just so committed to the roles." Ronald suddenly realizes his slip-up and attempts to cover. "Of ammunition; rolls of ammunition. That he fires into those targets. It's impressive."

Seething on the inside, smiling on the outside, Judith calmly responds and addresses him like a child, "This is why I told you not to invite him into your club, my dear."

"I thought it would give us an advantage! You know the saying, 'keep you friends close and invite your enemies to shoot guns with you," Ronald says, expecting Judith to laugh, but instead is met with a chilly stare. Suddenly, looking like a desperate man being interrogated by the police, Ronald pleads, "I want to hate him, but he's just so damn nice! And I'm not ashamed to say it, that man is handsome as the day is long. If he wanted to, he could not only be president of Altitude, he could be president of the United States of America. He just has that 'it' factor, you know?"

Judith stares at him in angry silence, then replies, "Are you finished?"

"I mean, I had a whole state of the union speech that I wrote for him if you want to hear it. I've always seen myself as a power behind the throne kind of a guy," Ronald says with pride.

Judith slaps the look of pride right off of Ronald's face and lectures him with angry curled lips as Ronald massages his cheek. "Listen to me, Jack is a snake who slithered his way into Madison's pants, married her just so he could rise in the company and now is preventing the board from doing the right thing. He's not a leader. He's a conman. And you know how I know all that? Because you told me every word that I just said. Not to mention, he isn't just blocking Altitude from going to some faceless company, he's blocking it from going to Lucid Corp., the company that I work for. Me, the woman who you supposedly love and trust."

"Boopie, you know I love and trust you." Ronald leans in for a kiss and is left hanging.

Judith continues, "You know what else you said? You said the whole reason why Art and Jack are blocking the sale is they think they're protecting Altitude's workers. Well, when Art isn't there to babysit everyone and Jack's incompetence drives the company into the ground, those workers will be laid off and their retirement will be flushed down the drain. Not to mention all the stock in the company that you've worked so hard to acquire."

Ronald sighs. "You're right. I'll get you guys the files; I promise. But what if that doesn't work? Am I still on the hook for more leaks?"

"First off, it will work. And even if it doesn't, our boss has other contingency plans that don't involve you."

"Good. Because the guy threatens to kill me every time we have a conversation. Haven't you told him I only swore that oath to get in your pants?"

"I have, but he takes the oath very seriously. Honestly, the fact that you don't take it seriously only makes him less likely to let you out of it."

"Wonderful."

Judith feigns guilt. "Are you mad at me?"

Ronald looks in her eyes and melts. "No, it's just… Back when we were dating you said it was a series of networking events that would help open up career opportunities for me."

"And that's exactly what it was."

"Okay, but then I win that raffle on the last day and suddenly we're in a mansion and everyone's wearing black hoods and performing weird rituals with all that fake blood; or was it real? Don't answer that. But you had that sexy black dress on and when I said yes to them, I thought it was to go into a private room for fun with you, but instead we get thrown in a coffin and now if I don't do things for the boss, I get killed. And really, does it have to be 'Big Jim?' Can't it just be Jim? I don't even know how big he is because every time we meet, I get blasted in the face with a spotlight. You know what, I'll bet Jim's not even his real name. I'm going to—"

"Honey, you're doing your panic rambling again."

Ronald takes a deep breath and nods.

Judith looks deeply into his eyes and says, "I am so sorry for dragging you into this. I truly thought this would just be a fun way for you to advance your career. I had no idea it would get to this level, but you're almost to the finish line. Just hang in there and trust me, Lucid Corp is a great company. Yes, they may have unusual methods, and actually Big Jim is not who we've been talking to lately, I don't know exactly who it is, but regardless, everything they do is for the greater good of humanity and their shareholders. Let's just make sure Altitude is in the right hands. Our future children are counting on you."

After hearing Judith reference children, Ronald smiles like a kid on Christmas morning. "Wait, children? I thought you didn't... You really want to have my babies?"

Judith presses her body up to Ronald's, softly caressing his neck and whispering into his ear, "Finish the job and I'll give you anything you want."

After delivering her directive, Judith gives her husband a seductive kiss before sauntering out of the room, leaving Ronald aroused and alone.

★★★

Emmy and Lance seamlessly work together converting the upstairs guest room into her home office. As Emmy unloads the final box of office supplies, she gets a call from Hank, informing her that he needs them to come out to the driveway. Emmy and Lance head downstairs and out the door as Hank pulls up and parks in the driveway in a brand new, black Chevy Suburban. Hank opens the door with pride, exits the vehicle and proclaims, "Feast your eyes on the Emmy-mobile!"

"Wait, really?! Are you serious, Dad?!" Emmy shouts with glee and almost tackles him with a hug.

Hank puts on a fatherly demeanor and warns, "Now, this ain't a gift. This is an investment in your business and I expect to see a return on my investment."

Emmy nods. "Of course, of course, what kind of a percentage do you want?"

Hank laughs. "Percentage? I don't want a percentage, Darlin,' I just want you two to make enough money to move out of my damn house."

Hank and Emmy share a laugh as Lance whispers to himself, "I pray for that every day."

Emmy gives Hank another hug and says, "Thank you so much, Daddy. It's beautiful, right Lance?"

Lance hems, "Well, it's not the most environmentally friendly vehicle."

Emmy ignores Lance's lack of enthusiasm as she joyfully hops into her new ride and takes it for a spin.

Hank tosses Lance a car fob and says with pride, "I had a feelin' you'd say that, so I figure'd I'd offset her carbon footprint with that bad boy right there." Hank points to a silver Chevy Spark EV Hatchback parked across the street. "I had the boys at the dealership drop it off over there. Don't want any of my neighbors thinkin' I drive that. Honestly, I'm surprised they let people take little things like that on the highway."

Lance stares in awe at the tiny car. "Well, you may not like it, but I think it's perfect. I don't even know what to say. That's so generous, Hank."

"Well, don't get ahead of yourself, it's a lease. I just couldn't in good conscience let you ride that rickety old bicycle around in our Texas heat."

Lance walks over to the car and notices a bumper sticker on the back that reads: "DALLAS COWBOYS #1 FAN," then looks back at Hank who howls with laughter. Lance shouts across the street, "Joke's on you Hank, they're going to charge you an arm and a leg to take that off!"

Hank, still howling, shouts back, "Worth every penny! And I ordered you matching plates!"

Chapter Seven

Day 101 of Pregnancy (Continued)

D usk settles in as Lance pulls his miniature electric car into the DFW Gun Range parking lot and parks in between two gargantuan lifted trucks. Lance takes a deep breath, exits the car and enters the lobby. He takes stock of his surroundings, surprised by its upscale feel, with pristine hardwood flooring, plush leather couches and impeccably organized guns lining the walls and filling the well-lit glass cabinets. A hulking African American man in his mid-fifties with a cuddly disposition greets Lance from behind the counter. "What can I do for you, Sir?"

Lance, still processing his unfamiliar surroundings, replies in a daze, "Wake me up from this nightmare."

The hulking man laughs and points to a nearby hallway. "Ronald's group is in classroom three."

"What? You just assume I'm not here to shoot? For all you know, I could be looking to purchase my next firearm to test at your range," Lance says, jokingly offended.

He laughs again. "I didn't mean to offend. Ronald showed me your picture and wanted me to make sure you went to the right room. Also, that little toy car you drove up in was a dead giveaway."

Lance nods in agreement. "Yeah, I guess any car that gets over ten miles per gallon sticks out like a sore thumb around here." He offers his slender hand to the giant, "I would tell you my name, but so far I've yet to meet someone who didn't already know it, so I'll just ask you what your name is."

The man's thick, powerful hand grasps Lance's. "My name's Andrew, but everyone calls me Tree."

"Tree... Well... Nice to meet you, Tree. As you know, I'm Lance, but everyone calls me hydrangea."

Tree lets out another bellowing laugh and says, "Looking forward to having you in the class. Soon as my co-worker gets back from his break, I'll head in."

Lance replies in shock, "You're in the class?"

Tree nods. "Go easy on me, I'm new to this whole acting thing."

"I typically make it a rule to go easy on anyone who is twice my size and has access to hundreds of guns, so you have nothing to worry about."

Inside classroom three, Ronald, back in his mock turtleneck, writes on the white board: "WELCOME LANCE FORD" as a slideshow with photos of Lance acting or directing in previous plays is shown on the adjacent instructional television. Five rows, with two small tables on each side and an aisle in the middle, line the narrow classroom. Ronald turns with anticipation as the classroom door opens and Lance enters. He greets Lance with a bow and says, "Ciao Maestro!"

Lance responds in perfect Italian, "Oh basta, non sono un maestro, al massimo sono un attore mediocre."

Ronald stares at Lance with confusion and says, "Sorry, I don't speak French. But it's so great to have you here! I brought you some cheddar cheese as a thank you." Ronald winks at Lance and hands him an envelope of cash. "I hope it's a Gouda amount!"

Serving that primal instinct to appease a man who hands him money, Lance forces a laugh at Ronald's cheesy joke as a tall, thin, bearded man in his early seventies with a striking resemblance to Willie Nelson enters the room, greets the two men and quietly takes his seat.

A few minutes later, three muscle-bound goons in their late twenties, with almost identical haircuts and skin-tight blazers, burst into the classroom and take seats in the back without greeting anyone. Lance looks askance at the goons and whispers to Ronald, "Who are they?"

Ronald whispers back, "They work for my wife's company. Nice guys, but a little reserved. I'm trying to get them to come out of their shell, but they have a bit of a temper."

Lance is about to question further, but realizes he doesn't really care and gives up.

Tree is the last person to enter when Ronald looks down at his phone with frustration and addresses the silent classroom, "Alright everyone, Jack just texted me that he and Andres are going to be late," Ronald turns to Lance like an agent talking to their diva celebrity client, "I'm so sorry about this, I told everyone to be here on time, but Jack clearly thinks he's better than us, so we'll just get this thing started. First off, let me welcome the man who needs no introduction, the toast of the legendary San Francisco theater scene... Lance Ford!"

Lance is greeted by a respectful round of applause from everyone except Tree, who cheers for Lance like he's at a football game. Ronald continues, "Thank you for your enthusiasm, Tree. Everyone else, give Lance the respect he's due, Capiche?" Ronald leans in to Lance and whispers, "That's Italian."

"Ah, good to know, thank you," Lance replies in faux appreciation.

Ronald continues, "So, here's the plan for tonight: Lance will lead us in some physical and vocal warm-ups, then each of you will come up to the front of the classroom, introduce yourself to Lance, tell him who you are, what you do for a living and how and why you joined the club. You'll then deliver your monologue and Lance will give you his feedback. Depending on how long it takes Jack to arrive, we may fill the rest of our time with some improv games. Sound good? Good. Okay, everybody up! Let's roll those tongues and wiggle those rumps!"

Emmy sits in the driver's seat of the Emmy-mobile, eyes locked on the entrance of Altitude Airlines' sprawling corporate headquarters. She glances at the dashboard clock, it reads: "8:05." She looks around at the nearly empty parking lot and says, "This guy really does work late."

A few minutes later, two men exit the bright, expansive lobby. Emmy pulls out her binoculars and identifies one of the men as Art's son-in-law, Jack, a strikingly handsome man in his mid-thirties with olive skin, a thick head of short brown hair and a dangerously infectious smile. The kind of guy who looks like he could be on the cover of both GQ and Men's Fitness. Following close behind Jack is an impeccably groomed Latin man in his late-twenties with an average build, clad in a tight, black Tom Ford suit and red velvet loafers. Emmy quickly flips through her dossier and confirms the man to be Andres Fernandez, Jack's longtime assistant. Jack and Andres walk together to two sparkling Tesla Model S's, one red, one black, backed in side-by-side. Emmy looks impressed and says, "Wow, it sure pays to be his assistant," as Andres hops in the red one and Jack hops in the black one. Emmy allows both cars to exit the lot before firing up her engine and following Jack at a safe distance.

After a few minutes of tailing Jack, Emmy pulls into view and sees Jack's car following close behind Andres' car; a few minutes after that, Andres pulls into the garage of a well-kept two-story house in a meticulously manicured subdivision. As Andres cuts his engine, Jack pulls into the garage and parks next to him. Emmy drives by and peeks into the garage as the door begins to close then does a loop around the block and parks within view of the house with her engine still on. She looks again at her dossier and confirms that Andres owns the house they entered. Her interest is suddenly piqued when she notices in the file that Andres is openly gay. Emmy muses, "Does Jack have a thing for his handsome assistant? Or are they just friends?"

Moments later, the garage door opens and the red Tesla with both men inside, pulls out of the driveway and speeds off. Emmy immediately takes off in hot pursuit, calmly saying to herself, "Ah, the ol' car switcheroo. Sorry, boys, that's just not going to work. Time to find out what Jack's been up to every Friday night."

Despite not having her tracker, Emmy easily keeps the red car in sight and tracks them to their destination: DFW Gun Range. She watches them from across the street as they park in the back lot and head into a hidden entrance to the building; a sight that leaves her visibly shocked and somewhat disappointed that her secret love-affair hypothesis is quickly evaporating.

After making a note, she pulls the Emmy-mobile around to the front of the building and her jaw drops at the sight of Lance's Spark parked near the main entrance. Her surprise quickly turns to joy as she pumps her fist and starts to giggle uncontrollably while swinging her car around and parking across the street from the Gun Range. As her giggles calm, Emmy smiles and whispers, "Well, Lance, you just might have a job with me after all. My sweet secret agent."

★★★

Lance sits alone at a middle table, pen and notebook at the ready, as he braces himself for the oncoming marathon of bad acting. Ronald, forehead perspiring from performing the warm-ups wearing his heavy cashmere turtleneck, stands in front of the class and says, "My name is Ronald Kozlowski and I will be playing the role of Willy Loman from *Death of a Salesman,* by the great Arthur Miller."

Lance sarcastically whispers to himself, "Gee, this is a new one."

Ronald takes a deep breath, closes his eyes and sits down in the chair behind him. After a very long pause, Ronald opens his eyes, stands up and delivers the monologue with surprising skill, looking every bit like a professional actor, except for the cashmere-induced sweat that drips down his face. Ronald uses his sleeve to wipe his sweaty forehead dry as he powerfully delivers the final line of his monologue, "*Today, it's all cut and dried and there's no chance for bringing friendship to bear or personality. You see what I mean? They don't know me anymore!*" Ronald closes his eyes, sits back down in the chair, takes a deep breath and says, "Scene!"

The class offers a muted applause, except for Tree who gives a Nature Boy-esque "Woo!" and a boisterous standing ovation.

Ronald stands up, looking very pleased with himself, as Lance smiles and nods from his seat. "Well done, Ronald. I think that's the four thousandth time I've seen someone do that monologue, so I wanted to hate it, but I gotta say, that was actually quite enjoyable. What experiences were you drawing upon for that role?"

Ronald fights back tears of gratitude. "Well, first of all, I just want to thank the gun club for their support. This was definitely for you guys. I want to thank my parents for teaching me how to lie. I want to thank my wife—"

"This isn't the Oscars. Just answer my question," Lance interrupts.

Ronald rubs his sleeve over his entire face, wiping away tears and sweat. "Sorry, it's just, hearing one of the greatest playwrights in America compliment my acting was overwhelming. What was the question?"

"I don't even remember at this point. Why don't we get the next person up there?" Lance says, looking around the room for a volunteer.

Ronald continues, "Oh yes, my experiences! Well, as the head of sales for Altitude, I understand the mind of a salesman. Also, I'm probably going to die at some point. Well, we're all going to die at some point, but there are times when I feel like it might happen sooner than later for me."

Ronald suddenly is lost in a daze. After a few moments of awkward silence, he snaps out of the daze, does a quick jig and sings, *"Or maybe I'll live forevaaaaah!"*

"Alright, thank you, Ronald. Who would like to go next?" Lance asks.

Tree raises his gargantuan hand. "I'll go!"

Lance nods at Tree who stands up, gives Ronald a forceful high-five as he walks to the front of the room and says, "Alright, well, you already know me, I'm Tree. I'm a part owner of the gun range. When Ronald told me what he needed the classroom for, I mentioned that I've always wanted to be an actor and he invited me to join. I'm not a professional like Ronald though, so don't judge me too hard."

"He's not a professional either," Lance says reassuringly.

Ronald laughs a little too hard and points at Lance. "You got me good!"

Lance ignores Ronald and asks Tree, "So, what have you prepared for us?"

"I'll be playing the role of Big Daddy from *Cat on a Hot Tin Roof,* by Tennessee Williams," Tree says. After a quick stretch, Tree takes a deep breath and delivers a riveting performance. Lance looks on in awe as Tree's booming voice fills the classroom with his final line, "*I've lived with mendacity! Why can't you live with it? Hell, you got to live with it, there's nothing else to live with except mendacity, is there?*"

Lance leads the class in an enthusiastic round of applause and says, "Wow! Tree, I know professional actors who can't do what you just did. That was incredible. Is this your first time acting?"

Ronald jealously mumbles, "Well, it wasn't *that* good."

Tree puts his hand to his heart and says to Lance, "First off, thank you, Partner. That is one of the nicest things anyone's ever said to me. And I've actually been an extra in a couple movies and I did some small parts in my high school plays, but football took up most of my time in those days and I didn't exactly come from a home that supported the arts. Mostly, my training just comes from watching a lot of movies."

"Well, keep watching them because you are spectacular. Who's next?"

The Willie Nelson look-a-like stands up and says with a lilting voice similar to his avatar, but a little bit deeper, "I'll go if that's alright with y'all."

Tree gives Willie a big hug and says to Lance, "This man is an incredible Willie Nelson impersonator."

Lance laughs, thinking it's a joke, but Willie stands in front of the class and says to Lance, "Tree is correct. I've been doing Willie Nelson tribute shows for the past few years and I just legally changed my name to Willie Nelson."

Lance attempts to hide his bewilderment as Willie continues, "I met Ronald when his wife took him to a networking event I was hired to perform at. We started talkin' after my set and he said he saw that I was good with the songs, but I was strugglin' to really inhabit Willie with my movement and speech and all, so he invited me to join this club and I definitely feel like my performin' is improvin'."

Lance smiles politely and says, "That's great. What will you be performing?"

"Well, seein' as there ain't no ladies in the group, I figured I might do a little gender bendin' and try my hand at playin' a female part just in case our play needs a lady. I can't shave the beard, but I think some makeup could cover that up or maybe it could be a bearded lady thing, I'll leave that to the experts, but tonight I'll be playin' Queen Gertrude from *Hamlet,* by William Shakespeare."

"Oh, boy..." Lance whispers to himself as he braces for the performance.

Willie goes into a soft falsetto with a faint British accent and says with difficulty, "*Drown'd! O, where? There is a willow grows aslant a brook, that shows his hoar leaves in the glassy stream.*"

As Willie continues to struggle through his monologue, he is gifted a merciful interruption by Jack and Andres loudly entering the classroom.

Ronald stands up in frustration. "Damn it, Jack! Willie was just gettin' to the best part!"

"Oh man, I'm so sorry, Willie. Please, continue," Jack replies guiltily as he and Andres find seats at a back table.

Lance seizes the opportunity to change Willie's course and interjects, "Actually, let's try something. First off, seeing Willie Nelson do Gertrude might be one of the weirdest and most amazing things I've ever witnessed.

So, thank you for that. But you said your goal was to improve your Willie Nelson act, so let's do an exercise for me. I want you to talk to Tree as if he's your pal, Waylon Jennings. I want you to tell Waylon about a really tough gig you just had. And I'm sure you've had some tough gigs that you can draw upon."

Willie looks unsure. "So, okay, well, uh Waylon, a couple weeks ago I got hired to perform at a sweet sixteen birthday party. The mom and the birthday girl had seen me a while back at the county fair and they were big fans. Unfortunately, the daughter's friends were not," Willie's confidence grows as the crowd laughs and he loses himself in the story, "Now, all I had with me was my acoustic guitar, and it ain't like Willie Nelson has a lot of electric rips, so I'm pickin' and croonin' and ain't a soul is listenin' except the Dad, but that's just cuz he's grillin' up the food right next to me. And let me tell you, singin' downwind of a charcoal grill is not exactly the best thing for the vocal cords, especially when you're havin' to sing over thirty-five conversations. The icing on the ol' birthday cake came when, and you may remember, we had that sunny day that suddenly started rainin,' well that was smack dab in the middle of my set. Now my guitar's wet and I'm worried my amp is goin' to short out, so I unplug everythin' and move it inside. We get in there and a couple of these kids start helpin' me wipe down the equipment and set up in the livin' room. I'm thinkin', these are some nice kids, then they ask for my auxiliary cable, I hand it to them and they plug a phone into my system and start blastin' hip hop, effectively endin' my set. But you know what, I still got paid the same amount, that Dad cooked up some real deal steaks and don't tell the feds, but I got some free weed out of it too. In the end, it always works out for Willie Nelson."

Tree pumps his fist and cheers loudly as the class applauds Willie, who nods with gratitude and says, "Thank you, that was mighty fun. You really are good, Lance."

As Willie returns to his seat, Andres stands up and confidently strides to the front of the room before Ronald can pick the next person to go.

Andres turns and smiles at Lance. "My name is Andres, I joined this club at the invitation of Jack Lorenzetti, the most amazing boss in the world, who pays me overtime to take this class and pursue my passion. Working for Jack at Altitude has been a life changer."

Chills run down Lance's body as he realizes the man sitting behind him is the target of Emmy's investigation.

Andres continues his introduction, "The character I will be portraying for you tonight is Faris, from *Good Night, Mrs. Bernstein.*" Andres closes his eyes, does an elaborate stretch and abruptly begins his passionate monologue about unrequited love, with his eyes directed at the wall and his emotions directed at Jack. "*I hate you because I can't be with you. I hate you because I can't talk to you. Because I can't touch you.*"

The further Andres gets into the monologue, the more overtly sensual and emotional his performance becomes. Ronald looks back at Lance and fans himself like an incredulous Southern Belle. Andres moans and delivers his final line, "*I knew if you were still standing at the point when my lips touched yours, it was only because I was holding you up.*"

Andres bows as the class applauds. Ronald rushes up to Andres and fans him like he's on fire, then looks over at Lance shouting, "Bet you never saw anything like that in San Francisco, Lance!"

Lance ignores Ronald and says to Andres, "Wow. Man. That was steamy. Now, I love how emotionally connected you were to the character, but what I think I'd like to see you work on going forward is diversifying your emotions within the text. There were a few beat shifts in there that I think you could have accentuated. I want you to really dig in and find ways to keep the performance unpredictable. If you don't do that, it can end up feeling a little one-noted."

Ronald interjects, "Whoa, who invited Simon Cowell to the club? Let's keep it positive, Lance."

Andres waves off Ronald and says, "No, I want the truth. Don't ever sugarcoat things with me. And I will do what you said, thank you, Lance."

"My pleasure," replies Lance as Andres glides back to his seat.

Ronald turns and points to the goons in the back of the room, "Would any of you boys want to go next?"

The goons shrug, stand up in unison and strut to the front of the classroom.

Ronald says meekly, "Guys, we're doing monologues not scenes tonight."

"My name is Brent," the first goon says, ignoring Ronald.

"I'm Rob," says the second.

"I'm also Rob, but people call me Knucks," says the third.

"What brought you guys to the club?" Lance asks with a genuine mix of curiosity and confusion.

"We met Ronald at a networking event. He was there with his wife. She's smokin' hot," Knucks says.

"Okay, moving on," Ronald says nervously. "Did you prepare a scene?"

"We were just going to say our favorite lines from *Super Troopers*."

"That's not even a play! The assignment was a theater monologue!" Ronald protests.

Lance interjects, "Relax, Ronald. We're not Julliard. Let's get back to why you joined the club. You met through Ronald's wife…"

Brent answers, "Yeah, we all got hammered with Ronald at a couple networking events and then Judith asked us to join Ronald's club and keep an eye on him."

"She didn't want me getting too carried away with the guns."

"No, she knows it's an acting club," Rob says.

Ronald's eyes go wide as he shouts, "She does?!"

"Let's stay focused, shall we?" Lance says as Ronald stares at the wall in shock. Lance continues, "Do you guys have any interest in acting or is this just a favor to Judith?"

"No, we want to act, but like, we want to do movies," Rob replies with nonchalance, hoping to conceal the fact that he actually is interested in acting and avoid Brent and Knucks' hazing.

"Movie actors get all the ass," Brent adds with a confident smirk.

Ronald whispers to Lance, "I'm sorry you had to hear that."

Lance ignores Ronald and, completely unaware that he's speaking to three hardened criminals, sharply replies, "Actually, in most cases, theater actors are considerably more promiscuous than film actors, but that's neither here nor there. Movies have monologues, so if you really want to be in them, you need to know how to do them. Learn one and stop wasting our time."

"He didn't mean that guys," Ronald says, attempting to protect Lance.

"Naw, that was real. I respect that. We'll work on it," Rob says earnestly as Ronald lets out a sigh of relief.

A puzzled Knucks looks over at Rob. "We'll work on it? What are you talking about?"

"I mean, you know, so we can get more broads. Like Brent said," Rob replies as the three men head back to their seats.

Before Knucks can question Rob further, Ronald stands up, turns to the class and says, "Alright folks, that's it for tonight."

Lance frowns and asks, "What about Jack?"

"Sorry, we ran out of time. Tree needs us out of here by eleven P.M.," Ronald says.

"You can stay 'till midnight for all I care. I want to see Jack's monologue," Tree says authoritatively.

Jack flashes his million-dollar smile and walks to the front of the room as Ronald sits down in defeat, pulls out his phone and looks at scantily clad photos of Judith in an attempt to divert his attention away from the impending performance and not be swayed by Jack's wiles.

"Hi, I'm Jack. A while ago, I mentioned to Ron that I was nervous about speaking in front of Altitude's shareholders. Later, he pulled me aside and told me about the club. He said it could help with my stage fright, so I gave it a shot and it definitely has, but honestly, I had no idea how much fun it would be. I've always been so focused on my career, so to have this kind of outlet has been like therapy. I just can't wait to surprise my wife with our play."

Despite his best effort at distraction, Ronald is touched by Jack's introduction and rushes up to give him a big, sweaty bear-hug.

Chapter Eight

Day 102 of Pregnancy

The dashboard clock reads 12:03 A.M. as Emmy watches Jack pull into the three-car garage of his sprawling Tudor house. She stifles a yawn and continues her conversation with Lance over her car speakers. "So, Ronald really paid you six hundred dollars?"

"Cold hard cash. Which is why I couldn't tell you. He swore me to secrecy."

"Well, I'm happy for you, but you shouldn't lie to me for any amount of money."

"I know. I'm sorry. I'll never do that again. Oh, and by the way, he offered me five grand to direct their play."

"Five grand?! You better take that gig," Emmy says as she begins her short drive home.

"Oh, I'm taking it. They might even do one of my plays, but hey, for five grand I'll direct *Legally Blonde: The Musical.* Plus, they're shockingly good. I mean, not all of them, there's these three super creepy meatheads in it, but I think it's going to be a great cast."

"See, I knew you'd love Dallas!"

"Don't get ahead of yourself. I still have to wake up at the butt crack of dawn tomorrow to go golfing with a psychopath. And your brother is drunkenly snoring on the couch again."

"Cuddling him didn't work?"

"Keep up the jokes and I might have to change my mind about being your secret agent. Honestly though, I think that Jack guy is clean. His assistant is in love with him, but who could blame the guy? Jack's like a young Clooney without the terrible nineties hair."

Emmy laughs. "So, you don't think there's anything going on with those two?"

"I'll keep you posted, but it seemed pretty one-sided to me."

"Well, this is shaping up to be a pretty easy first case."

Ronald closes the garage door behind him and quietly enters the house. His phone buzzes with a text from Judith that reads: "Meet me in the office." Ronald puts down his gun bag, walks upstairs and opens the office door to find Judith wearing a see-through negligee. Ronald wipes the drool from his mouth as Judith sensually catwalks over to him, gives him a passionate kiss and whispers, "Unlock those files and we'll play while they print."

Lust vibrates through Ronald's body as he whispers back, "It may take me some time to access them from home."

Judith slowly runs her fingers down his body. "I'll be waiting…"

The picturesque golf course sparkles in the early morning sun as Lance sits sleepy-eyed in Hank's golf cart and watches Principal Dwyer ready his driver for the first tee. Hank walks over to Lance holding two drivers and says, "You can't hit the ball from that cart, Son. Let's get you up now, ya hear?"

Lance gingerly rises out of the golf cart and takes one of the drivers from Hank, saying, "This is the tee time you're so worried about keeping?"

"You're damn right it is, we're doin' eighteen holes. That's about four hours. You start any later than this and you'll be sweatin' your ass off by the sixth hole."

Lance nods in agreement as they walk over to the tee and stand beside his gun-toting next-door neighbor, Art, who looks at Dwyer with contempt. Art whispers to Hank, "Why in the Sam Hell do I have to be on that weasel's team?"

Hank whispers back, "He's already pissed at me enough as it is; if I'm the reason he loses to Lance, I might as well start golfing at a public course. Plus, he's scared of you, he ain't scared of me."

Art grumbles as Dwyer tees off with impressive power, sending the ball sailing onto the green. He turns and walks with swagger towards Lance, saying, "You know, Lance, the only man I've lost to in the last five years was my dear friend, Tony Romo. The very man whose name you dragged through the mud in my office. Now, I don't know if you're aware, but many golf analysts have said that he is such a naturally gifted golfer, that if he wanted to, he could've been better than Tiger."

Art looks at Dwyer with disdain as he steps to the tee. Just as Art takes his swing, his cell phone rings, causing a slight hitch that sends his ball sailing out of the fairway. Art curses as he fishes the phone out of his pocket and answers, "Jack, it's Saturday, take a day off, would ya?"

Art's demeanor suddenly turns grim as Jack informs him that there was a data breach last night and Altitude's new interior design and technology-infusion plans for their fleet were compromised. Lance attempts to get close enough to hear Jack, but is unable. Art sighs and says into the phone, "This is why I hate all these damn gizmos. Anyone can take your stuff. I'll call you later, but soon as I finish this round, I'm goin' to find out who did this, I promise you that."

Art hangs up the phone and says to Hank, "Don't ask. Just take your shot." Hank nods, walks over to the tee and delivers a drive on par with Dwyer's.

Lance places his ball, readies himself and takes a big swing that barely grazes the ball, sending it a few yards in front of him. Dwyer lets out an evil cackle and says, "Whoa, who invited the scratch golfer?"

Lance swallows his pride, ignores Dwyer and marches over to his ball, taking another sloppy hack that sends it a little further this time.

Over the next four hours of golf, Lance slowly gains his golfing sea legs. That, combined with Art's lack of focus due to the breach, keeps the game shockingly close. On the eighteenth and final hole, Art shanks multiple putts, leaving Lance putting for the win. Dwyer menacingly paces around the green hoping to distract and intimidate Lance, who takes a deep breath and smoothly taps the ball toward the hole, but narrowly misses it. Dwyer pumps his fist and taunts Lance who walks over to his ball, kneels down to read the putt, stands up, hits the ball and misses again. As Dwyer celebrates his victory, Art walks over to him with a look of disapproval and says, "Act like an adult."

"Sorry Art, that boy needed to be taught a lesson and I am glad I got to do the teaching," Dwyer replies, about to continue his celebration when a loud text notification on his phone quickly turns his joy to annoyance.

"Everything alright, Champ?" Hank asks.

"Yeah, it's just one of our alumni. You remember Tree Robinson? He played D-Tackle at UT," Dwyer says.

Lance interjects, "I know Tree, he's awesome."

The three men look at Lance with suspicion and Dwyer says, "How exactly do you know Tree?"

Lance suddenly remembers the secrecy of the club and says, "Uh, I was at his gun range last night... Shootin' them pistols."

"You've never shot a gun," Dwyer replies, in full interrogation mode.

Art intervenes, "Put a cork in it, Dwyer. Lance is tellin' the truth, Ronald invited Lance into his gun club and they shoot at Tree's."

"Guess again," Dwyer hisses.

"You better watch your tone, Dwyer," Art warns.

Hank jumps in, hoping to cool the temperature. "Whoa there, why don't we just head to the grill and have some lunch?"

Dwyer persists, "No, I'd like Lance to tell us what he was actually doing at the gun range or else I'm going to turn down the favor that Tree asked of me."

Lance sighs. "Alright! Jeez, what is your deal? Ronald's gun club is actually a secret theater club and they want me to direct their first play."

Art looks genuinely shocked as Dwyer smiles with satisfaction and says, "Thank you."

"So, Ronald lied to me?" Art asks Lance.

Lance senses the note of hurt in Art's voice and calmly replies, "He was just embarrassed and wanted the whole play thing to be a surprise."

Dwyer cuts back in, "You know, Tree asked if they could use our theater, but since they have such a disreputable director, I have no choice but to turn him down."

Dwyer's pettiness takes Art's mind off of Ronald and stirs his inner Papa Bear. "Before you make any decisions, Dwyer, I just want to ask you a question, have you been enjoyin' those free first-class upgrades you and your wife keep gettin'?" Dwyer nods, suddenly realizing he's about to be check-mated. Art continues, "It would be a shame if you had to explain to Sheila why you're suddenly flyin' everywhere in coach, wouldn't it?"

"Yes, it would," Dwyer grumbles through gritted teeth as Lance and Hank joyfully look on.

"And I don't need to remind you that Emmy is my one and only goddaughter and Lance here is very special to her, which means he's very special to me and you know how much it means to me when a man helps my loved ones. So, I hope you will continue to enjoy your upgrades and not only grant him access to your theater, but reconsider him for that teaching position."

Dwyer forces a smile and says, "Okay, they can have the theater, but I already hired a drama teacher so I can't help you there. Although I will say, I only hired the guy out of spite, he's not even a drama teacher, he's a football coach, so if I like the play I'll consider giving Lance the job next year."

"That's the spirit. Now, if y'all will excuse me, I got to go handle some business," Art says with a wink as he playfully pats his revolver, hands his caddy an exorbitant tip and drives his cart back to the clubhouse.

Dwyer watches him speed away with frustration then gives his caddy a meager tip and sulks back to his cart.

"Is Art's whole thing an act or is he for real?" Lance asks Hank, still in awe of Art's domination of Dwyer and dramatic exit.

"All real. Why do you think Dwyer's so damn afraid of him?" Hank says as they hop into the cart and drive back to the clubhouse.

"I just figured it was the gun."

Hank laughs. "You could be armed to the teeth and Dwyer wouldn't be afraid you. It's the man behind the gun that scares him. And by the by,

I want to thank you for missin' those last couple putts. I don't want you to think I'm goin' soft, but I know you did that intentionally and I really appreciate it."

Lance smiles at Hank, truly touched. They reach the clubhouse and the warm mood is swiftly crushed when Duke emerges from the building dripping with sweat and rushes up to the cart, jumping on the back and rocking it like King Kong.

"Damn it, Duke! Get the hell off my cart!" Hank shouts.

Duke hops off the cart, puts his sweaty arm around Lance's shoulder and says, "Man, you should have seen the rack on this new student in my spinning class. I couldn't focus, Bro. Every time I looked up to lead the next phase, I'm starin' straight at those things."

Lance slips out from under Duke's arm and wipes his shoulder with disgust. "Sorry, as much as I'd love to continue this stimulating conversation, I'm late for lunch with Emmy."

"Actually, you're early for lunch with Dad and me. I just talked to Emmy and she said she has to go meet with a client, so you're all mine, Yoga-Boy! I just gotta shower real quick. It's like a rain forest in my undercarriage."

★★★

Emmy checks her surroundings as she walks over to a shaded park bench and sits down facing the shimmering White Rock Lake just a few feet away. She pulls out of her purse a children's berry juice box, one of the few liquids she can keep down, and quenches her thirst. A few minutes later, Art walks to the bench, sits down next to Emmy and fills her in on the news of the day. Emmy shakes her head and asks, "Do you have an idea who's behind the breach?"

"Our tech guys are doing forensics on it, but so far there's no trace of who did the hack. All they're tellin' me is it had to come from inside the company. And whether or not he's responsible, that project was Jack's and if those files end up in the hands of Delta or United, the board will be out for blood."

"Well, speaking of Jack, I know what he's been up to," Emmy says as she hands Art a folder.

"Well, you work quick my dear," Art says, opening the folder and thumbing through pictures of Jack entering the gun range with Andres and later, exiting the range deep in conversation with Ronald and Lance. Art shakes his head and says, "He's in that damn theater club?"

"You know about it?"

"Just learned about it this morning. Lance told me."

"You gotta be kidding me. It's supposed to be a secret!"

Art replies with a chuckle, "Calm down my dear, he didn't want to. Dwyer forced it out of him, but he didn't give Jack up. And I'm tellin' ya, that Lance is one kind, patient hombre. I'd have slapped the snot out of Dwyer if he talked to me like that, but your man took it on the chin for Hank."

Emmy smiles at Art with gratitude. "Well, he spoke highly of Jack and at least so far, I'm not finding anything incriminating. I do think he should have told Madison about the theater club, but I guess he wanted it to be a surprise. And judging by the breach, my gut tells me there are people who want Jack to fail."

Art nods pensively. "You know, when I started Altitude, I spent the first five years locked in court battles with the big corporate airlines that were tryin' to choke us out of the industry. Now, here I am ready to retire and the same kind of corporate hacks are tryin' to steal the company. It didn't work then and it ain't goin' to work now. My internal guys will do their investigations and I'll make sure you get every bit of info. Just promise me you'll stay under the radar. I don't want anything happenin' to you and that baby."

"Happening? What would happen? Isn't this just corporate espionage?"

"When you're dealin' with money at this level, it can cause people to do some pretty horrific things. Just promise me you'll be safe."

★★★

Judith stands in the pitch-black hotel room and squints her eyes at the blinding spotlight. After a very long minute, the same mysterious cowboy voice breaks the silence. "Ronald may be a buffoon, but his hacking skills are impressive. I hear he didn't leave a trace."

"I told you he'd come through," Judith replies.

"You were right. And Chet'll give you a handsome bonus on your way out, but your work ain't done, Sweetheart. When those files are delivered to every major airline, Jack will take a hit, but we need a knockout blow. We need your target to be killed."

"I know. I have a master plan."

"Who needs a master plan? This ain't rocket science. You just tell Knucks and the boys to kill the guy, plant some evidence on Jack and be done with it."

"But Jack has no motive."

"He doesn't need a motive. He doesn't even need to be charged. Just the suspicion of murder will have the board runnin' scared. By the time he's cleared, we'll have sealed the deal."

"Why not make it really easy and kill Jack?"

"I may hate Art, but I'm still old school. You leave the family out of it. I ain't goin' to make his daughter a widow if I don't have to. Just stick to the target and keep it simple with Knucks."

"You've gotten so boring. Is the Altitude money really that important that you can't have a little fun?" Judith playfully replies, hoping to conceal the fact that despite her ambitious drive to succeed, she would rather not submit a nice man like Lance to the kind of grisly murder that her boss has a penchant for.

The cowboy relents. "Fine, tell me your idea, Little Lady."

"My idea is for Jack to shoot Lance without even knowing he was doing it. Ronald and his little club are going to put on a play and he wants to do a murder mystery that Lance wrote. He said in it there's a shooting and he wants Jack to play the role of the murderer. All I have to do is convince Ronald to cast Lance as the person being shot by Jack, swap out the fake gun for a real gun and bam, a theater full of people will watch Jack shoot and kill a man in cold blood."

The cowboy laughs uproariously at Judith's idea. "You are one crazy vixen, I'll tell you that. I just don't see the need to wait that long for a plan with so many contingencies."

"Some things are worth waiting for. Especially when your would-be hit men are sloppy oafs like Knucks, Brent and Rob. You think those guys really know how to plant evidence? And you know I'm not getting my hands dirty for this one. Plus, it'll give us time to see if the design leak works. Maybe the board will oust Jack and we can save a life."

The cowboy grunts, "I hate to say it, but that's a pretty damn good point. We'll do it your way, but I want a ticket to that show."

The spotlight shuts off, leaving Judith in complete darkness.

Chapter Nine

Day 103 of Pregnancy

Lance, Emmy, Lupita, Duke and Hank sit around the kitchen table eating breakfast. Emmy and Lupita wear fancy dresses and Hank is dressed in his favorite blue suit; attire that is in stark contrast to Duke and Lance, both still in their pajamas.

"You really are welcome to come with us to Mass, Lance," Lupita gently says.

Emmy cuts in, "Forget it, Mama, he's a lost cause."

"I'm not a lost cause, it's just... Not really my thing. I always feel out of place. Inevitably, I stand when everyone else sits and then I do the wrong hand motions and it just gets embarrassing."

Lupita shoots Emmy a stern look. "You don't guide him, Hija?!"

"I go over it with him literally every Mass he's been to. He can memorize four thousand yoga poses, but kneeling twice is too much," Emmy replies.

Lance puts his hands up in playful defense. "Hey, I was fantastic at all the rituals during our wedding ceremony, though. Everything the priest told us to do, I was on it. But Mass is different. There's more pressure."

Emmy looks confused. "More pressure than our wedding?"

Lance shrugs as Duke pats him on the back like an old comrade and says, "I'm with you, Lance, I went to Catholic school and I'm still lost half the time. Plus, I'm a free thinker like you. I don't need someone teaching me how to be a good person. I just naturally am, so why go?"

"It's about more than just being a good person, Hijo, it's about a relationship with God," Lupita says.

"Me and God are cool, Ma. In fact, when you guys are in church, God's gonna be chillin' with Lance and I as we guzzle a twelve pack and watch some golf," Duke says with swagger.

Lance shudders at the thought of Duke's plan and seeing it as his only excuse to avoid Duke, searches for a way to justify his sudden interest in Catholicism. "Wait, do you guys go to that big stone church down the road?"

"Yep. Christ the King. And let me tell you, I've pumped a whole lot of money into them stones. I could've had a new boat, but no, gotta help out the ol' Padre," Hank complains then braces himself for a whack on the arm from Lupita.

Lance continues, "Well, I'm a real Cathedral design aficionado, so I'd love to see the inside and soak up the holiness within those walls."

Emmy laughs and rolls her eyes at Lance's Duke-induced interest in the faith. "Back in San Francisco, we had one of the great architectural masterpieces in the nation at Saint Dominic's and you never once had any interest in going."

Lance innocently shrugs and says facetiously, "God works in mysterious ways. Who are you to judge my faith journey?"

"Lance is right, Hija, you need to welcome the stranger. Lance, we'd be honored to have you. Now, go put on your suit."

Lance scrunches his nose and says, "Oh, uh, I actually don't own a suit..."

Lupita looks shocked. "You don't own a suit? What do you wear to important occasions?"

"I usually just put on some jeans and a button up. The closest thing I have to a suit is the tuxedo from our wedding," Lance says with a smile.

Lupita nods, "That will do."

Lance forces an uneasy smile at the prospect of wearing a tuxedo, but his tuxedo qualms are squashed when Duke interjects, "Come on! You'd really rather look like a penguin in church than kick back some tall boys with your bro?"

★★★

Art and Jack stand at the front entrance of Christ the King Catholic Church handing out bulletins and greeting every parishioner by name like friendly politicians. Jack looks debonair as usual in a tight, designer suit and Art, true to form, wears a vintage suit, bolo tie, cowboy hat and boots with a pistol strapped to his waist. With no new entrants in sight, Art turns to his son-in-law and says, "I don't need any excuses and I ain't mad, but you should have told Madison about that theater club."

Jack's perfect skin goes pale. "Oh no…"

"Relax. I ain't goin' to tell her, that's up to you. I have it on good authority that you wanted to surprise her with it and improve your performance at work. So, I'll take your balls out of the vice I initially wanted to put them in," Art pauses and smiles as he holds out his hand to an approaching elderly woman. "Maybelle, you look younger by the day."

She laughs and pats Art on the arm. "It's all those free trips to Maui you keep giving me."

"I'll keep 'em comin', just don't tell that Jack guy over there, he thinks I give away too many freebies," Art says with a wink and ushers her inside. Alone again with Jack, Art continues their conversation. "Obviously, this little thing with Ronald is a nothin'-burger, but as a top-level executive, you're goin' to have a whole heck of a lot of offers to join a variety of secret groups or clubs or societies or whatever you want to call them. My rule is if it's secret, it's dangerous. Even this little club you're in now was startin' to cause problems. Madison's all worried that you might be runnin' around on her, so now I'm thinkin' this ain't the guy I thought I knew. All because you made some stupid pact with Ronald; and don't you worry, I'm goin' to have a chat with him too."

"I'm really sorry, Art. Seriously. And please, go easy on Ronald. He's a good guy and I've gotten a lot out of the club," Jack says soberly.

"I'll be nice, but just promise me no more secret clubs. Don't join 'em and don't fight 'em. Just do your job, serve your company, serve your family and serve your God. Got it?"

Jack gives Art a solemn nod. "I promise."

A steady flow of parishioners approach in the distance as Art looks down at his watch and says, "Alright, it's ten minutes to noon, get ready for the rush."

Hank and Lupita hold hands as they walk along the sidewalk and turn onto the main church walkway with Emmy and a tuxedoed Lance few paces behind them. Art greets Lupita with a kiss on the cheek before she and Hank enter the church. As Emmy and Lance approach, Art takes stock of Lance's shiny black tuxedo and says, "Whoa there, Partner! This is a church service not a Sinatra concert."

Lance begrudgingly laughs and is about to sling a witty comeback, but notices the gun strapped to Art's waist and his mind goes blank.

"Be nice, Art. He wore it at our wedding, remember?" Emmy says with a nudge.

"Ahh, how could I forget? That was a beautiful day. And I'm just playin' with you, Lance. Thank you for comin' and thank you for dressin' the part," Art says, giving Lance a friendly elbow to the arm.

Jack adds, "I think you look awesome, Lance. Here's a bulletin."

Lance nods with gratitude and takes the bulletin as he and Emmy enter the church vestibule. Lance looks around and says to Emmy, "Where'd your parents go?"

"They're already seated. If Mom is ten minutes early, she's late, so I'm sure she booked it up to the front," Emmy says as she dips her finger in the Holy Water font, crosses herself and leads Lance into the sanctuary.

Lance looks around in awe at the intricate, high-domed ceiling and large stone pillars lining both walls as he follows Emmy up the middle aisle. As they make their way, Lance notices Emmy's parents are seated front row-center and a self-conscious shudder runs through his body. He says to Emmy, "Hun, I can't sit in front looking like this."

"Stop. You look great."

Lance sighs as they sit down next her parents. Lance looks at Lupita, deep in prayer, and whispers to Emmy, "Is that like, some sort of pre-game ritual?"

Emmy shushes Lance and he protests, "What? It was a legitimate question. Also, can we talk about Art bringing a gun to church? Is this a place of worship or the O.K. Corral?"

Emmy stifles a laugh and whispers back, "Art is head of security for the noon Mass."

"I'm no biblical scholar, but I don't recall Jesus ever packin' heat."

"Well, I feel safer with him armed."

Lance persists, "Countless studies have proven the 'good guy with a gun' theory wrong. Once in a blue moon it works, but the numbers don't lie."

"Yeah, except Art is a more accurate shot than ninety percent of the police officers I worked with. Your academic studies don't account for his level of skill," Emmy whispers and ends the conversation with a glare.

Lance shrugs, unconvinced. The congregation stands as the choir begins the entrance hymn. Lance leans in and whispers to Emmy, "So, when am I supposed to kneel again?"

★★★

The hot afternoon sun shines on their newly tiled backyard pool as Judith sunbathes on a luxurious, custom-made chaise-lounge, wearing a skimpy black bikini and drinking a mango piña colada. Ronald stands nearby, examining the row of rosebushes lining the fence with a look of dissatisfaction as sweat begins to soak through his unflattering tank top. He looks over at Judith and says, "I'm not sure the gardeners really know how to properly prune. Do you know if they're sealing the fresh cuts?"

"I tell them every time," Judith lies, completely disinterested.

Ronald squats down to examine the roses closer. "Well, they sure aren't listening."

Judith sucks down the last of her drink and says, "Bartender, I'll have another!"

Ronald rushes over to Judith, takes the glass, walks over to the outdoor bar and mixes her another drink.

"Thank you, Love," Judith says as Ronald hands her the glass. She takes a sip through the straw. "So, I read *Purple Sky*. I think it's the perfect play. Lance really is a talented writer and you were so smart to hire him."

Ronald's eyes suddenly begin to water as he says, "That is so wonderful to hear. It means the world to me that I can share my passion with you and I'm so sorry I didn't tell you sooner."

"It's okay, I should have said something when the guys told me about it, but I didn't want to make you feel self-conscious," Judith says. After pulling Ronald in for a kiss, she adds, "I would love to help you cast the play if that's alright."

Ronald looks uneasy. "I'll have to run it by Lance, he is the director and you know how those industry types can be."

Judith looks confused. "You're paying him though. Doesn't that make you the boss?"

"Of course, I'm the boss," Ronald replies, feigning confidence.

"Well, then you should be able to cast whomever you want," Judith says with a smile then sucks down another gulp of booze.

"You're right. I'm calling the shots and if my wife wants to be the casting director, well then she's going to be the casting director."

"That's right! Now, like you mentioned, I agree that Jack should play the role of the bad cop who shoots his partner."

Ronald bites his lip. "I was actually kind of thinking I would play that role."

"No, no, no, I can't bear to watch my hubby play a murderer," Judith says, stroking Ronald's cheek.

A flattered Ronald smiles and says, "So, you think I should be the hero cop?"

"No, I also can't bear to watch my hubby get shot," Judith says with loving sadness.

"It's just acting, I won't actually get shot," Ronald protests.

"I'm sorry. I can't have it. Plus, you need to play the role of the funny bakeshop owner. He's the anchor of the whole play and no one will be able to bring the kind of laughs that you can."

Ronald sighs. "You're right. You can't waste a comedic genius like me. So, who should play our tragic hero?"

"Lance."

"Lance? But he's the director."

"Why can't he do both? You said he's done it before and if anything, I think he'd be flattered you asked."

Ronald thinks it over and says, "Okay, I'll check, but I don't know if he'll want to."

Judith sucks down the rest of her drink. "Remind me again who the boss is?"

He puffs out his chest. "I'm the boss!"

"That's right! Now, go make me another mango piña colada."

"Right away, Sweetheart," Ronald says before subserviently taking the glass and shuffling back to the bar.

★★★

At the conclusion of the Mass, Lupita stays behind to pray as Hank makes his way to a nearby pew and boisterously greets one of his clients. Lance looks over at Lupita and whispers to Emmy, "She's really committed."

"Don't make fun of my mom," Emmy warns.

"I'm not making fun of her; I think it's inspiring. She's like a Zen master. Maybe if you had that kind of commitment to your faith when we met, I would have joined the flock years ago," Lance says with a wry smile.

Emmy shakes her head, ushers Lance into the aisle and walks him out of the church where Art and Jack are once again standing with friendly smiles and an armful of bulletins. After some pleasantries, Art hands Lance his stack of bulletins and pulls Emmy aside for a private conversation. Lance hands an exiting elderly couple a bulletin as they point at his outfit and give him a thumbs up. Lance turns to Jack and says, "You know, I always thought Catholics were kinda grim, but everyone here is so nice."

Jack laughs, "Well, they better be, they don't have much to be grim about in this community. But considering there are a billion Catholics, odds are you're going to get all kinds."

"I just don't get why I can't have the bread and wine."

"Gotta be prepared."

"Listen, all my stand ups, sit downs and kneels were perfect today. I'm prepared, Baby."

Jack says with a chuckle, "Nope. You gotta do at least a year of classes."

"Whoa! A year?! In that amount of time I could just learn how to make the bread and wine myself."

Art and Emmy stand in the shade of a large tree out of earshot. Art shakes his head and says, "Jack just got a text from his buddy at United. They have the files."

"It was United?"

"No, Ma'am. They received it anonymously. And I'll bet by the end of the week Delta, American and just about every other airline in the country will have 'em too. This is still about one thing, underminin' Jack so the board can sell."

"And you have no idea who this shadow company they want to sell to is?"

"I have my suspicions, but the ones who would tell me don't know, and the ones who know wouldn't tell me."

Emmy laughs. "I've never met anyone who can stand up to an Art interrogation."

"The people they're beholden to are way above my raisin' and there's nothin' I can threaten 'em with that's worse than what'll happen if they let it slip."

"There's gotta be a weak link."

Art looks up at the church, takes a deep, pondering breath and says, "Karl Torlakson. He's our only shot. You dig up enough on Karl and he might crack."

Chapter Ten

Day 106 of Pregnancy

Emmy wears a long, conservative summer dress and floppy hat over a blonde wig with heavy makeup caked onto her face as she walks swiftly through the lobby of the Cirque downtown high-rise apartment building. She's followed close behind by Lance, clad in a short-sleeve white dress shirt, blue tie and black slacks with thick glasses and a fake goatee. His right hand grips his cell phone in camera mode and his left clutches *The Book of Mormon*.

They approach the elevator. Emmy presses her keycard to the sensor and the doors open. Once inside, she presses the button for the 26th floor then the close button. Lance leans in and says, "This is such a rush. I love it, my first undercover sting operation! And how did you get that key card? You're amazing."

"Hun, relax."

"Sorry. Right. Gotta be cool. Cool as a cucumber. That's me. Mormon Joe," Lance looks down at Emmy's slightly protruding baby bump and smiles. He leans down and says to her belly, "Your mommy is one amazing detective."

"Thank you. But seriously, I need you focused."

"Aye aye, Captain," Lance says and goes quiet until they reach the 26th floor, where the doors open to a pristine, sunlit hallway with a view of downtown Dallas. Lance looks around in awe. "Man, it really pays to be a mistress these days. Whatever happened to cheap hotel rooms?"

"Is that where you house all your mistresses?" Emmy says with a sarcastic wink, then shushes Lance as they reach their destination: room 2614. She takes a deep breath and rings the doorbell.

Karl Torlakson, wearing nothing but a bathrobe, opens the door, his eyes bloodshot from a steady flow of wine and weed. He pauses for a moment, then greets them with confusion. "Can I help you?"

"Hi, my name is Margaret, this is my husband, Joe," Emmy says and motions to Lance who gives a nerdy wave. Emmy continues, "We were just wondering if we could talk to you real quick about your faith."

Karl sighs. "Oh, good God."

"Yes, He is a good God," Lance replies earnestly.

A woman's voice from inside the apartment yells, "Karl, who's at the door?"

"Aw, is that your wife?" Emmy smiles and peaks inside at an attractive woman in her twenties, wearing just a bra and panties.

An inebriated Karl slowly looks behind him to see if she is visible from the doorway and says, "It's the Mormons again."

Lance immediately snaps pictures of Karl and his mistress, then hides his phone just before Karl looks back at Lance and Emmy and asks, "How do you people keep getting into the building?"

"Karl, are you familiar with The Church of Jesus Christ of Latter-day Saints?" Emmy replies.

"I am familiar and I am not interested in your god or any other god," Karl says.

As he begins to close the door, his mistress walks up behind him, now wearing a thin satin robe. She smiles at Emmy and Lance, looks them up and down and says, "Wow, they're cute. You guys swing?"

Karl looks dumbfounded at his lover as Lance sneaks the lens of his phone just over the top of his book and snaps a photo of them.

Emmy reaches into her purse, pulls out a prayer card and hands it to Karl. "You'll find some great information there."

Karl hands the card back to Emmy and says, "No, I won't. Please leave."

"God bless," Lance replies with a smile and wave goodbye as he and Emmy walk down the hall.

Emmy whispers to Lance, "Stay cool until we get back to the car."

"I'm a cucumber, remember?" Lance replies.

After taking the elevator back down to the lobby, exiting the building and hopping into the Emmy-mobile, Lance pumps his fist and let's out a loud, "Wooo!"

Emmy laughs and takes off her wig as Lance says with excitement, "What a freakin' adrenaline rush, Babe! You were amazing! Like, I would never want you being an undercover cop, but you're a damn good one."

"Let's see the photos," Emmy replies, still in work mode.

Lance pulls up the pictures on his phone and shows them to Emmy who smiles with pride and says, "Beautiful work! I think it's safe to say these photos, combined with the dirty real estate deals we uncovered yesterday, are plenty of ammo for a Torlakson take-down."

"Man, my wife is hot."

Emmy gives Lance a naughty smile. "You know, we are in the second trimester, this is the time to have some fun before things start getting dicey."

Lance shakes his head. "One week on the job and I'm already sleeping with my boss."

Emmy laughs. "You know of any cheap motel rooms?"

Duke paces the free weight area of the Royal Oaks Country Club gym and stares at himself in the mirror with satisfaction before lifting two heavy dumbbells and pumping out a set of bicep curls. As Duke finishes his set, he glances over at Judith, clad in skin-tight workout clothes, bouncing with each stride on an elliptical machine. Duke increases the volume and intensity of his workout, hoping to get Judith's attention, but she keeps her eyes locked on the TV suspended from the ceiling. On it, a report from a local newscast discusses the high-profile leak of Altitude's new plane design. After finishing his set, Duke walks over to Judith with a little too much confidence, leans on her elliptical and says, "You still in the market for a personal trainer, Beautiful?"

"No. And don't call me beautiful," she replies, keeping her eyes on the TV.

"Yeah, probably for the best. All my clients end up falling in love with me and I wouldn't want little ol' Ronald gettin' jealous."

"As much as I love getting hit on by men I wouldn't touch with a ten-foot pole, I'm going to have to ask you to walk away before I file a sexual harassment complaint," Judith says with her eyes still on the TV.

Duke attempts to maintain a veneer of confidence, but it's obvious her shot at him was effective. He glances over at the TV and reads the closed captions, perking up at the opportunity for more conversation. "Ah I see, you're stressed about those leaks. Well, rest-assured, Emmy's goin' to find out who did that."

Judith's blood runs cold at the thought of Emmy's involvement. Suddenly, Duke is a much more interesting conversation partner. She fakes a smile and says, "That's so great. I didn't know she was working for Altitude now."

"I probably shouldn't talk about it. She didn't even tell me, I just overheard her talking to Lance, but yeah, I guess Art hired her. And my sister may be annoying, but she's damn good at investigatin' stuff."

Judith continues her fakery. "That's wonderful."

Duke attempts to seize on Judith's shift in demeanor. "Any chance I can change your mind about the personal training? I promise I'll be a good boy."

Judith gives a flirty smile to her new font of information and says, "You know, I could use some tips on my strength training. We'll start with that, and if I like you, we'll expand the workouts."

"Rad," Duke says with a wink.

"Don't say rad," Judith replies.

Duke nods. "Never again."

★★★

Judith lies down on their plush living room sectional couch and watches The Food Network as Ronald returns home from work looking exhausted. He greets Judith with a kiss and asks, "What's for dinner, Doll-Face?"

"Well, Bobby Flay just made the most amazing grilled Mahi Mahi dish. Can you make us that?"

Ronald laughs uneasily. "We don't have any Mahi Mahi."

"I'll Google the recipe and you can go get everything from Tom Thumb."

Ronald wearily shakes his head. "Sorry, I'm not up for it." He makes a poor attempt at an impression of Bilbo Baggins, saying, "*I feel thin, sort of stretched, like butta' scraped ova' too much bread.*"

Judith looks shocked at Ronald's uncharacteristic refusal of her whim and passive aggressively says, "Okay then…"

"Sorry, it's just been a long day. This leak has created a mountain of work for us. And I'm hearing that the board still isn't budging."

Judith feigns sympathy. "Yeah, and unfortunately, I have more bad news. Art hired Emmy to investigate the leak."

"No…" Ronald says as chills run down his spine.

"That's what I heard from Duke."

"Duke? Is he involved?"

"No, he's just an idiot who happened to overhear a conversation. News of the leak was on at the gym so he brought it up."

"Ah, does your boss know?"

"Not yet, but don't worry, just stay calm and I'll take care of everything. You've done your part."

Ronald's expression grows dark, "He better not touch Emmy. If she gets harmed in any way, I'm goin' Rambo."

"Wow, I've never seen you so protective about anyone. Not even me. Should I be jealous?"

"Don't be ridiculous. She's like family. Hank's the one who got me the Altitude job when I was waiting tables at the country club, so yeah, I'm going to protect them. Not to mention, she's pregnant."

Judith laughs. "Relax, I was just messing with you. I love Emmy too and nothing is going to happen to her."

"Thank you," replies Ronald as he slumps down on the couch next to her.

Judith snuggles into Ronald's arms and says, "Can we talk about something more fun? Like the play?"

"Of course. Did you put out the casting notice for our female lead?"

"No. That's what I wanted to discuss. What if I were to cast myself in that role?"

"Really?! You want to?!" Ronald replies, excited at the prospect of working with her.

"Yeah, I think it would be fun. It's been a while since I've acted, but back in my modeling days I did a bunch of commercials and every director said I should have moved to Hollywood."

Ronald exclaims, "This is wonderful! We're like Brad and Angelina!"

"Aren't they divorced?"

"Right. We're like Ted Danson and Mary Steenburgen!"

"Eek, they're a little old, don't you think?"

"Oy, it's just a metaphor. Okay, Ryan Reynolds and Blake Lively!"

"Bingo!"

Ronald's face drops as it dawns on him that her character will be in a love-triangle with Jack's character. He sighs and says, "Just don't fall in love with Jack."

"Stop. You know I can't stand him."

"Yeah, but it's Jack. That smile. Those eyes. Ugh, I may not be cut out for this whole Hollywood power couple thing."

Chapter Eleven

Day 107 of Pregnancy

L upita comes home from Thursday morning Mass with a look of concern. She walks into the living room where Lance is doing yoga on the floor and Emmy is hard at work on her laptop. They greet Lupita and she somberly replies, "When I prayed for Lance this morning, I saw gran peligro around him."

Lance sits up from his pose, looks at Emmy and asks, "Peligro? I don't know that word."

"Danger," Emmy replies.

"Danger? Did you get any idea where the danger is coming from?"

Lupita shakes her head. "Unfortunately, I did not."

Lance rolls his eyes. "Just my luck."

Lupita pulls turquoise Rosary beads and a prayer card from her purse, hands them to Lance and says, "Use these to pray to La Santa Madre and then we are going to buy you a suit."

"A suit? How's a suit going to protect me?"

"The suit is to look proper when you go to La Misa and pray that God will protect you."

"Lupita, I love you, but this is a little out of left field," Lance replies as she gives him a stern look. Lance raises his eyebrows and says, "Yikes, that's the look you give Duke... I see why that's so effective."

Emmy chuckles. "Yeah, no one can stand up to that glare."

Lance acquiesces. "Okay, I'll do what you say. Guess it can't hurt."

Lupita nods in approval and says, "Good. And after suits, we will go to my favorite café. I called and they have your vegan blueberry scones."

Lance replies with excitement, "Free clothes and a blueberry scone? This is my kind of danger."

★★★

Once again, Judith finds herself standing in the pitch-black hotel room as the blinding spotlight is turned on. After a long silence, the cowboy says, "The leak didn't work."

Judith sighs. "Did anyone flip?"

"Oh yeah, the damage was done, but there's one or two swing votes hangin' by a thread for Jack. When can I expect to attend that play?"

"I don't know. Ronald says they have a venue, but it's the North Dallas High Auditorium and apparently the principal is a bit of a prick."

"Well, I don't care if he's Joseph Stalin. I want it done in a month."

"A month?! They can't pull off the play in a month."

"That's the point. It'll be utter chaos backstage, which will make your job easier."

Judith bites her lip and nods. "Good point. Okay, a month it is." After a long pause Judith says, "There's something else. Art's goddaughter has been hired to investigate who's behind the leak."

"Okay? So, Art gave a little girl a summer job. If she's as dumb as his real daughter we have nothin' to worry about."

"She's not dumb. I know her. And from everything I've heard, she's a brilliant investigator. And she's Lance Ford's wife."

The cowboy clears his throat and spits in frustration. "This is what I get for having a heart. I didn't want to kill Art's son-in-law and now I may have to kill his goddaughter."

"Let's take it easy. I'll keep an eye on her. If she gets too close, I'll let you know, but we should be fine. She's not doing any employee interrogations and Ronald's work was spotless," Judith says, genuinely hoping to protect Emmy.

The cowboy cackles. "Yes, it was. That little twerp is smarter than I thought."

Judith ponders for a moment and asks, "If I may be so bold, why does this Altitude deal mean so much to you? Every other takeover has been low-hanging fruit; greedy men just dying to sell their souls for profit margin. I know Ronald was an easy way in, but Altitude is filled with boy scouts. You had to know it was going to be a struggle."

Silence fills the room as the cowboy takes a few moments to ponder and says, "I own an oil company, a media company, multiple food chains, a toilet paper company and have a large stake in twenty-seven other large companies across just about every business sector. The same losers who complain that Lucid Corp has its hand up the ass of half the puppet politicians in the country, are usin' my oil to fuel their cars, are watching TV shows I funded, are eatin' at restaurants I own and when that food they eat comes out the other end, they're usin' my paper to wipe. I can count on one hand the men in this country that are as powerful as I am and every one of the millions of insignificant sheep out there should be kissin' the ground I walk on.

"But I don't let that happen. I'm smart. Very few people know who I am. I have no title at Lucid. I'm a shadow. When those losers complain, they complain about Big Jim. As if Big Jim has any power whatsoever as CEO. Even you, one of my shrewdest operatives, met me and hadn't the faintest idea who I was.

"Ah, but Art, he knows who I am. We were very close in our youth. No matter what he did to me, I stuck by him. Even when he married the only woman I ever loved; I still forgave him. One woman is meaningless in the grand scheme of things, but she was some woman. And in the 80s, when he started Altitude and I bought my oil company, I told him my plan for Lucid. I offered him free entry into the network. He didn't even have to do any rituals. But no, he thought he was better than that. Better than me. He even had the balls to tell me I needed to change my ways. He talked to me like I was a child. That was the last time we ever spoke to each other.

"From that day on, I waged a silent war against him. At the time, we had a couple airline CEO's in the network and I made sure they locked Altitude up in a decade of legal battles. From there I took a couple silent runs at buying the company. I wanted to take the company and turn it into everything he hates, but he fended off each takeover. He was smart enough to keep his company, but too stupid to ever know I was behind it. But now I have him. He's old, he's tired and his company will be mine. I want him to spend his retirement watching Altitude turn into the profit machine that he never could create and to know that I did it. I won. I am the better man."

After a few moments of silence, Judith replies, "Wow, that sure clarifies things. You are definitely the better man. Thank you for telling me all that."

"I'm a sucker for a beautiful woman; especially one like you. I tell you what, if my pecker still worked, I'd be tempted to come out of the shadows and make you my wife."

Judith laughs. "Don't make me blush."

"But Judith, if you tell anyone a word of my story, there will be dire consequences."

"I wouldn't expect anything less."

The cowboy laughs and shuts off the spotlight off.

★★★

Art nurses a sputtering 1959 Philly-Mint Cadillac Coup Deville into his driveway, parking it next to his impeccably maintained red 1968 Shelby Mustang GT500. He leaves the engine running as he pops the hood and examines the engine in the fading sunlight. Out of the corner of his eye he sees Ronald tiptoe onto Hank's perfectly manicured lawn on his way to see Lance. He clears his throat, spits into the bushes and hollers, "Ronald! You got a minute?"

Ronald stops in his tracks, his heart racing as he forces a smile and turns to Art. "Of course," he replies and jogs across the lawn.

"We need to have a serious talk," Art says, faking a stern look at Ronald, who doesn't pick up on the joke and stares back in fear. Art continues, "Is there somethin' you ain't tellin' me?"

A rush of terror flows through Ronald's veins. He lets out a nervous laugh and barely catches his breath enough to ask, "What do you mean?"

"You know what I mean. Don't lie to me, Ronald. You know how I feel about liars."

Ronald attempts to respond, but his sudden panic attack leaves him unable to muster any words. Art steps forward and says, "Tell me. Right now."

"I really… I don't…" Ronald drops down to one knee and attempts to catch his breath.

"You all right, buddy? I was just bustin' your balls about that theater club," Art says, gently placing his right hand on Ronald's shoulder.

Ronald stares wide-eyed at the ground as he realizes they were having a completely different conversation. He wipes away a tear, stands up, bows and puts on his best lying face. "I knew all along! Just wanted to show you my improv skills. Pretty convincing, right?"

Art busts out laughing. "Boy, you really had me goin', Ronald. You were sweatin' like a whore in church."

Ronald smiles with pride. "Thank you. The sweaty whore is one of my signature characters."

"All jokin' aside, I am genuinely curious as to why y'all didn't tell me in the first place? Jack had me thinkin' he was two-timin' my daughter and you had me thinkin' you could actually shoot a gun."

"Touché. I just, you know, you're such a man's man, and I can't speak for Jack, but I didn't want you and Hank to think less of me. You guys have been like the fathers I never had and I'm already a big enough wuss as it is, so I wanted it to be this big surprise like at the end of a movie where you guys come to the play and I blow you away with my talent and tearfully wave as my two dads give me a standing ovation," Ronald says, pondering for a moment the fact that he has double-crossed his father figure.

"Well, first off, I ain't marryin' Hank, so you can throw the two dads thing out the window, and second, I believe a real man does what he loves without shame. I'm lookin' forward to this play and I hope you don't ever feel like you can't be honest with me," Art says and offers his hand to Ronald.

Ronald shakes Art's hand with gratitude and for a split second considers coming clean about the leak, but decides against it and turns to leave. Before he can go, Art stops him and says, "By the way, I want you to take Fridays off until you're done with the play. Your pay will remain the same and you won't lose any vacation days."

"Are you serious?"

"Yeah, you've been lookin' real stressed the past couple weeks and I know how hard you've been workin' to control the damage from the leak, so it's the least I can do. Make sure you're fresh for the club," Art says as Ronald rushes up and gives him a bear hug. Art looks down and says, "Now, don't go makin' me regret that decision."

Ronald lets go with a nervous laugh and says, "Thank you so much, Art."

"My pleasure, I knew somethin' was up, because normally when I'm workin' on my cars, you come over and talk my ear off, but lately you've been like a ghost. And I'm sure that wife of yours is also runnin' you ragged."

Ronald's anxiety returns as he laughs nervously and says, "Yeah, that's it. That's why. She's a slave driver!"

Art laughs. "Aren't they all, Partner?"

Emmy is hard at work in her upstairs home office, digging into the transcripts of Altitude's investigative interviews with a look of frustration. She glances over at Lance who poses in front of the full-length mirror hanging from the door, examining the fit of his tight Ted Baker suit with a look of satisfaction. He turns to her and says, "I always thought suits were for corporate hacks, but I'm starting to see the appeal. I feel like James Bond. And your mom is a super cool lady. She told me about some of the things she and her family had to endure to come to this country. It was really inspiring stuff. We had a legit heart to heart."

Emmy offers a subdued chuckle. "I'm happy to hear it."

He looks at her with concern. "What's wrong?"

"It's these damn investigators. They're not asking the right questions and there's nothing I can do with this. I just wish I could be more involved."

He puts a comforting arm around her. "I'm sorry sweetie. Why don't we go down and get some hot cocoa? I'll give you a little massage."

Emmy nods as they gather up all the papers, lock them away in her filing cabinet and head downstairs where Ronald's smiling face greets them in the living room. Lance whispers to Emmy, "Now it's my turn to be stressed."

Ronald points a teasing finger at them and says, "Uh oh! What were you two lovebirds up to?" Emmy laughs off Ronald, gives him a hug and heads for the kitchen as he says to Lance under his breath, "You dog you. We're the same way. Judith and I can't keep our hands off each other. It's just pure animal magnetism."

Lance scrunches his nose in disgust. "Well, there goes my hot cocoa appetite."

Ronald over-laughs and whispers, "Is it different with the whole pregnancy thing?"

"Alright, well it was great seeing you, Ronald," Lance says sarcastically as he ushers Ronald to the front door.

"Wait!" Ronald says as he pulls ten crisp one hundred-dollar bills from his wallet and hands them to Lance who looks down with confusion. "What's this? You already paid me."

"I paid to license your play and hire you to direct. The extra thousand dollars is for your services as our tragic hero cop: Conor O'Hanlon!"

Lance thinks for a moment before saying, "I'm flattered, but don't you think Jack would be a better fit? He's almost exactly how I envisioned that character would look when I wrote it."

"No, he needs to be the crooked cop. No one will be expecting it!"

"Okay, but I still don't know if I'm up for it. I kind of left my acting days behind me."

"Yes, but you know this script like the back of your hand! And considering Conor has the most lines in the play and you already know those lines, it'll make it easier for us to pull off the play by June twenty-second," Ronald says, bracing himself for Lance's reaction to the date.

"What?! That's in a month! We still have to build the set, make the costumes, hire our tech crew, not to mention rehearse so we don't look like a bunch of fools. What's the rush?"

"First off, Tree is part-owner of a big construction company and he's already said he can get the set built in a week. As for the date, it's not my first choice either, but Judith has made it clear that she doesn't want the play interfering with our July travel plans. I didn't even know we had July travel plans, but apparently, we will be spending three weeks in Costa Rica. Also, speaking of Judith, I was thinking instead of holding auditions, let's save time and give her the role of Laura. She wasn't just a model; she was also a stellar actor. Word on the street is she could have been bigger than Scarlett Johansson if she wanted to! So, what do ya say?"

"I'm starting to wonder who the actual director is," Lance replies as Ronald pulls another thousand dollars and hands it to him. Lance looks down at the cash in his hand. "Congratulations, Judith, you got the part."

Ronald gives Lance an unwanted celebratory hug. "This is going to be the greatest play in Dallas history!"

A look of confusion comes over Lance's face as he halts Ronald's celebration and says, "Wait, I thought Judith wasn't supposed to know about the club."

"Yeah, that's out the door. Apparently, she knew all along."

Lance shakes his head. "So, no more secrets?"

"Of course not! We need to start promoting this thing. The North Dallas High Auditorium has a lot of seats to fill and Tree really went out on a limb for us with that Principal Dwyer guy. And from what I heard about your interview, I don't need to tell you twice what a nightmare that guy can be."

Lance breathes a sigh of relief as Emmy returns from the kitchen with two cups of hot cocoa. Ronald looks over at Emmy, takes the cup meant for Lance and says, "Thank you so much for the cocoa, Emmy! I was actually just about to leave, but why not? Let's relax and hang for a bit. I actually have tomorrow off so let's spend the day digging into those role assignments! I love it, we're a regular Rodgers and Hammerstein! Or should I say, Ronald and Lancerstein?" Ronald giggles at his joke and Lance musters up a joyless smile as it hits him how much time he'll be spending with Ronald over the next month.

Chapter Twelve

Day 108 of Pregnancy

E mmy pulls a purple maternity t-shirt and jeggings from her dresser, puts them on and measures her growing baby bump in the mirror. Lance enters the now fully moved in, impeccably clean and organized bedroom wearing nothing but a towel, his hair still wet from the shower. He walks over to Emmy, gives her a passionate kiss and says, "Don't worry, your belly is gorgeous."

She lays her head on his chest with gratitude. "I'm just so excited for our little nugget to come."

Their moment is interrupted as Duke pops his head into the bedroom and announces, "Yoga-Boy, my homies and I are goin' brewery-hoppin' around noon, you wanna come?"

"Isn't that a little early for alcohol?" Lance asks.

"It's not alcohol, Dude. It's just beer," Duke replies incredulously.

"Right. How silly of me. Regardless, I appreciate the offer, but I need to be sharp for rehearsals tonight."

"It's beer! What's the big deal? I'm teachin' two cardio classes right after."

"Well, you are an impressive man. I, on the other hand, am a lightweight. I smell beer and I get drunk."

"Whatever you say," Duke mutters and closes the door in defeat.

Emmy lowers her voice and says to Lance, "It really is cute how much Duke likes you."

"What? All the guy does is make fun of me."

"Exactly. That's what he does to people he likes. Plus, he keeps trying to find ways to hang out with you."

"I always just assumed they were traps."

Emmy laughs, "Duke isn't that smart."

After a few moments, Duke pops back in and says, "Sis, I forgot to ask, are you goin' to take any of my classes? Because you gotta make sure you keep off those L-B's." Duke pats his belly, turns to Lance and says, "I've seen so many of my clients became tanks after pregnancy. You gotta watch out for that, Bro. Her body may never be the same."

Emmy scowls at Duke. "You're lucky I'm prohibited from physical altercations because otherwise I would slap the piss out of you."

Duke laughs out loud and scampers out of the bedroom.

Lance shakes his head in disapproval and says to Emmy, "I'll love you no matter what happens to your body. Although, I will say, you should consider the pre-natal yoga. Not for your weight or anything chauvinistic, but some of the poses can really strengthen and stretch out the... Southern region... For the big push."

"The southern region?"

"I was trying to be delicate."

"Well, I appreciate all of the fabulous suggestions from you and my brother and I will take them into consideration. In the meantime, put some pants on your southern region."

Lance gives Emmy a sarcastic smile as he takes off his towel and slips into his boxer briefs. A split-second later Ronald opens the door without a knock.

"Really? The open-door policy extends to bedrooms?" Lance exclaims as he grabs a pair of pants and puts them on.

Emmy intervenes, saying, "Yeah, Ronald that's a bit much."

"Oops! So sorry! Duke said I should head right in," Ronald replies innocently.

Emmy sighs. "Of course he did."

Lance looks at the time on his phone and says, "Also, why are you here so early? I haven't even had breakfast yet."

"That's perfect! I haven't either! Let's get some sausage and eggs at Yolk," Ronald says.

"Ohhh, Yolk is so good!" Emmy says wistfully.

Lance shakes his head. "Sorry, I don't eat sausage and eggs."

"You'll love their oatmeal," Emmy says encouragingly.

"I can make oatmeal here," Lance replies, hoping she will get the hint that he doesn't want to go with Ronald.

Ronald interjects, "Come on, you can't have a big production meeting at a kitchen table! Everyone knows a proper showbiz meeting has to be done at a hip restaurant. Did you learn nothing from *Entourage?*"

Lance lets out a defeated sigh and says, "I guess we do have a lot to go over before tonight. I'll meet you outside."

"Huzzah!" Ronald exclaims as he points to the ceiling. "We'll be laughin' and yolkin' it up!"

Lance rolls his eyes. "Alright, now you really need to get out."

"What? That was funny! Like yuck it up, but yolk. Get it?" Ronald says with a shrug, gets nothing from Lance and whispers to Emmy, "these stars are hard to impress."

★★★

An inebriated Karl Torlakson walks slowly down the dimly lit hotel hallway wearing the same suit he's had on for two days. Chet greets him with a handshake, opens the hotel room door and follows Karl inside the pitch-black room. Just before the spotlight turns on, Chet puts on a pair of dark sunglasses and positions himself between the door and Karl, who curses at the blinding light and complains, "Damn, that thing is brighter than I remember."

"Karl, I'm hearin' some disturbin' things from your Altitude cohorts," the cowboy says menacingly.

"What're you talkin' about?"

"You're swearin' your allegiance to the wrong men. Art ain't your friend and when Jack gets done, he'll wreck the company and all you'll have left are those shady real estate deals I set you up with."

"I'm not swearing my allegiance to anyone. All I said was that Jack deserves a fair fight. I'd still be on your side, but that leak stunt was flat-out wrong. You shouldn't have to harm the company to win your battle. Fight fair and I'm back on your side."

The cowboy sighs in frustration. "What a time for you to gain a conscience. You didn't seem to have a problem with my methods when I made that drug charge disappear. Or when I paid off your gamblin' debts so your bookie didn't take off your legs. Or when I provided you with plenty of foreign buyers for your garbage condominiums. No, you never once said a damn thing about my methods then. So, what are we to do about you?"

The alcohol in Karl's blood can't hold down his sudden feeling of dread as he pleadingly replies, "Okay, you're right. I've been ungrateful. I'm sorry. It's been a stressful time and you know I'm protective of Altitude. That's why I was behind you as the buyer in the first place, because I agree, Jack is going to sink our stocks. I just thought the leak was unnecessary, but that was wrong of me to assume I knew better. So, I promise, I'm on your side and we'll have the votes and the company will be yours."

"I figured you'd come to your senses, but we still have a problem. In your fit of righteousness, you mentioned to your mistress that you wanted to spill the beans to Art. Not just about the takeover, but about our entire operation. That can't happen. Once we have Altitude, Art can know everything; in fact, I welcome it. But until then, he's dangerous and you know that. At this point you're more trouble than you're worth. Goodbye Karl."

★★★

The clock on the wall of the classroom reads 7:55 P.M. as Ronald finishes setting up a Bose tower speaker and nods at the club members who file in. After Lance returns from the bathroom, Ronald excuses himself, exits the classroom, and walks through the lobby to the firing range. As he walks down the row of booths, he waves to Judith who loads a Glock 19.

"You want a few pointers, my love?" Ronald asks.

Judith shakes her head with a smile, places noise-cancelling earmuffs on her head, takes a deep breath, positions her body with expert technique, aims her pistol at the gun range target and empties the clip. Ronald stares in awe as every bullet hits the bulls-eye. Judith takes off her earmuffs, turns to Ronald and says, "What were those pointers you had, Sweetie?"

"I had no idea you could shoot like that..."

Judith winks. "I'm full of surprises."

"You sure are. That was Lara Croft-level skill."

"Who?"

"You've never seen *Tomb Raider?* It's a classic!"

"Is that like *Indiana Jones?"*

Ronald shakes his head in disbelief. "We'll discuss this later. In the meantime, be ready for my text cue so we can do your big introduction."

Judith gives him a "thumbs up," then reloads her gun and returns to target practice as Ronald walks away, still in shock over her shooting skills and lack of film knowledge.

Inside the classroom, Lance greets Jack with a bro-hug as Ronald returns, walks to the front of the room and addresses the club. "Greetings everyone! Welcome to the first rehearsal for *Purple Sky.* It's a gritty crime drama set in 1950s Los Angeles about two cops who attempt to solve the infamous murder of a prominent financial advisor, murdered in a bakeshop on the wrong side of the tracks. As they follow the clues, both men fall in love with the bakeshop cashier, which drives one of the cops to do the unthinkable: kill his own partner. And best of all, it's written by our very own celebrity playwright, Lance Ford!"

Brent shouts from the back, "He ain't a celebrity!"

"I totally agree," Lance replies.

"But that story sounds tight. Did you get the idea from *Goodfellas?"* Rob asks.

"Goodfellas?" Lance replies with confusion as he searches his mind for any common threads between the two stories.

Ronald interjects, "Let's stay on track, shall we? I am so excited for this life-changing production. Now, everyone has a copy of the play in front of them along with Altitude commemorative highlighters and pencils." Ronald suddenly turns into a pitch man, adding, "Altitude, flying coast to coast, providing the best service in the business and unbeatable prices with no gimmicks. Altitude, for all your air travel needs."

Lance turns to the class and sarcastically says, "Ronald also has plenty of exciting timeshare opportunities if any of you are interested."

Ronald looks genuinely surprised. "How did you know that? I actually do. Lake Tahoe, Cabo San Lucas—"

Lance interrupts, "Keep it moving, Bubba."

"Yes, right. I am excited to inform you that Tree has secured us a venue and date for the performance. It will be at the North Dallas High Auditorium on Saturday, June twenty-second and we will be rehearsing Wednesday through Sunday evenings until then."

Chaos ensues as everyone in the room except Tree and Lance objects to how soon the play will be done. Ronald waves his arms to calm them down and shouts, "Lance will abridge the play to make it easier to pull off and if everyone commits to the rehearsals, we will be fine! Now, time to assign some roles!" Ronald grabs the microphone that is plugged into a nearby Bose sound tower and presses play on his phone. The Chicago Bulls' theme song by The Alan Parsons Project, booms from the speakers and fills the classroom with the iconic instrumental as he does his best sports announcer impression and shouts into the microphone, "Are you rrrrreeaddyyyy for the grrreatest theatrical production in Daaallaaaasss Historyyy?! First up, the man who will guide this production to the promised-land, playing the role of hero cop, Conor O'Hanlon…. Laaance Foooorrddd!"

Tree stands up and screams for Lance as the rest of the group applauds with varying levels of enthusiasm. Ronald motions for Lance to run up to the front of the class and join him and he reluctantly acquiesces.

"Next up, the Heartthrob of the Heartland, playing the role of Vincent Palladino, the traitorous cop who shoots his partner, O'Hanlon in cold blood… Jack Loooreennzetiiii!"

Jack does a smooth jog to the front of the class as Tree and Andres cheer enthusiastically and Ronald says into the microphone, "Man, he even jogs cool. Is there anything he cannot do folks?"

Andres shouts in admiration, "Nope!"

Ronald gives Andres a thumbs up and continues, "With that, let me welcome that handsome man who will be playing the role of Romero Guzman, coffee magnate falsely accused of the bakeshop murder, Andrrress Ferrrnnaandezzz!" Andres claps his hands to the beat as he jogs up to the front and does a Michael Jackson-esque spin move and pose.

"Whoa! Watch out Kevin Bacon, there's a new footloose man in town!" Ronald says as Lance rolls his eyes at the outdated reference. Ronald continues, "What's that? Are we at the country music hall of fame? No? Who's that man? That Blue-Eyed Stranger? He is one of our own and he is playing the role of Tom Wilson, the postman who overheard the bakeshop murder, so please put your hands together for Willllieeee Nelllsssoonnn!" Willie walks up and squishes into the increasingly crowded front of the classroom. Ronald points to himself and says, "And now, your producer and king of comedy, playing the role of Mr. Blankenship the owner of that fateful bakeshop, Ronnnaaaald Kozlowskiiiiii!" Ronald does a jig that accidentally unplugs the microphone and sends him tumbling into Jack, who skillfully catches him and holds him upright.

Ronald continues as though nothing happened, plugs the microphone back in and says, "Playing the suspicious bodyguards of Romero Guzman, we have The Muscles of the Midwest, Rob Breewwssterrr, Brent Brrrreckenriidge and Knuuckkksss Monticeellloo!" Ronald motions for the goons to come up to the front, but they ignore him and stay seated in the back, looking at their phones. Ronald says with a nod, "Probably couldn't fit up here anyway, that's very thoughtful of you guys... Okay! Next up, in the role of Police Sergeant, Bob Preminger, we have the local sports hero, Hercules of our hometown, a deadeye shooter with a heart of gold, the one, the only, Treeeeeee Roooobinnnsoonnn!"

"Woooooo!" Tree shouts as he rushes up to the group, high-fives everyone and gathers them into a huddle, leading them in a cheer.

When the cheer finishes, Ronald starts the entrance music from the beginning and says, "Alright, the moment you've all been waiting for: the ladies... Who will be joining our group? I will tell you who. Playing the role of Laura Marks, the bakeshop cashier whose rejection of Officer Palladino and love for Officer O'Hanlon causes Palladino to commit murder, will be played by former super-model and one-half of the next, great Hollywood power couple... My wife, Juddiithhhh Kozloowsskiiii!"

The goons in the back look up from their phones and ogle Judith as she opens the door to the classroom, catwalks to the front and gives Ronald a kiss on the cheek amid raucous applause. Knucks continues his objectifying stare at Judith and says, "She's so damn hot, Bro."

"Thank you, Knucks," Ronald replies with an uncomfortable smile.

Lance takes a peek at the cast list, chuckles and says, "Ronald, you're forgetting a character."

Ronald loses all of his enthusiasm as he shakes his head and says, "At the request of our director, we have cast in the role of Mrs. Blankenship, my character's wife... Willie Nelson. Playing two roles."

Everyone except Ronald cheers joyfully as Willie takes a bow and says to Lance, "I won't let you down."

Chapter Thirteen

Day 109 of Pregnancy

Duke wears a beige fishing outfit as he tiptoes into Lance and Emmy's room, both asleep in the early morning darkness. He stifles a giggle as he silently kneels down and whispers into Lance's ear in an attempt to mess with his dreams, "Hi, Lance, my name is Kandi, is this your first time at the strip club, Big Boy?"

Lance, still asleep, rubs his ear and shifts away from Duke, who stifles another giggle as he removes the covers from Lance's body and says, "Lance, what're you doin'?"

"I'm sleeping, go away," Lance groggily replies as he attempts to pull the covers back on.

"Dude, we gotta leave in fifteen minutes if we're gonna hit the lake by sunrise."

"What does that have to do with me?"

"You said last night you were coming with us!"

"I was being sarcastic."

"That's not how we took it. And my Dad's all juiced up to get the three of us out on the lake. You're really gonna disappoint him after he bought you that little granola car?"

"He leased it; but point taken," Lance says with a groan as he pulls himself out of bed and adds, "your mom better be right about that whole Heaven thing, because I'm putting in some serious work here."

"Don't worry, you're about to find out that Heaven is a lake full of fish, ready to be caught."

Lance wants to laugh mockingly at Duke's idea of Heaven, but can only muster a whimper. Once fully clothed, he looks over with envy at Emmy, who lies in bed, blissfully asleep.

★★★

The Sun peaks out over the horizon of the silent, sparkling Benbrook Lake. Hank sits behind the wheel of his four-seat fishing boat and preps two poles as Duke sits next to him, prepping his own pole and Lance sits in the back, swatting bugs.

"You alright there, Lance?" Hank asks.

Lance slaps his neck and says, "These mosquitoes are enormous."

"A beer'll keep 'em away," Duke suggests as he opens the ice chest, grabs two bottles of cheap domestic beer, pops the top on both and offers one to Lance who declines. Duke shrugs. "Suit yourself. You want one, Pop?"

"Heck yeah I do," Hank replies as Duke hands him a beer and they both take a swig. Lance lets out a loud yawn then groggily apologizes. Hank says with a chuckle, "You ain't a mornin' person, are ya, Lance?"

"This isn't morning, it's purgatory," Lance replies, mid-yawn.

Hank laughs and hands Lance a fishing pole, "I still can't believe you've really never been fishin' before."

"Nope. My parents were both hippies and I've just never had any interest in it. Still don't."

Hank shakes his head and says, "Well, that's a damn shame. When I was a kid, my Pappy, God rest his soul, made sure my brothers and I knew three things: how to catch a fish, how to treat a woman right and how to take a punch."

"He punched you guys?" Lance replies, suddenly disturbed.

Hank chuckles. "No, we punched each other. But if we ever got outta line, he'd whoop us a lil' bit." Lance smiles uncomfortably as Hank and Duke cast out their fishing lines. Hank continues, "I guess now that you're my son-in-law, I gotta teach you the same things."

Lance awkwardly attempts to cast out his line to no avail.

"Here, let me show you how it's done," Hank says and reaches over to guide Lance's arms as he casts out the line.

"That's more like it. Okay, next lesson: Duke, punch Lance."

"Wait, what?!"

Duke stands up and raises his fist as Lance attempts to shield himself. Hank and Duke bust out laughing. Lance shakes his head unamused. Hank says, "Just messin' with ya, kid. If the ladies found out I let Duke punch you, I'd be a dead man."

"Yeah, come on now, Yoga-Boy, you know I wouldn't hurt that pretty face," Duke says with a laugh as he sits back down and takes another swig of beer.

Moments later, Lance's fishing line begins to tug and he shouts, "I think I got something!"

Hank barks, "Okay, well set the hook and give that sucker hell!"

"I don't know what that means!" Lance replies.

Hank mimes a fast pulling motion and Lance acts accordingly. The line starts to pull.

"You got it!" Hank exclaims.

Duke watches Lance and says, "Don't screw this up, Bro!"

Lance clutches the reel and begins to turn it.

"Boy, that's a bigun'. Okay, nice and smooth, move that pole up and down and reel in it," Hank says, demonstrating with his hands.

Duke sees Lance begin to lose it and says, "It's almost gone! Give me the pole!"

Hank shouts, "Duke, stand down!"

The line begins to slack, Duke rolls his eyes and says, "See, he lost it."

"That's alright, you just gotta be a little smoother with it next time."

The line suddenly pulls violently. Lance nearly loses his grasp on the pole. Hank exclaims, "We're back in business! Remember, strong and smooth!"

After some struggle, Lance reels a large bass out of the water. Hank grabs the line and pulls the fish into the boat, skillfully removes the hook, drops it into a large bucket of water and says, "Addaboy! Look at the size of that thing! Whaddya say, Duke, is Lance officially a real man?

Duke laughs. "Nah."

Lance rolls his eyes as Duke playfully rabbit punches his shoulder and says, "Now he is."

Lance grabs his shoulder in pained silence and drops down on one knee. Hank looks on with pride. "Welcome to the family, Lance."

After a few moments, Lance shakes off his shoulder pain and looks with pity at the bass swimming in circles. He stretches out his dead arm one more time before grabbing the bucket of water, dumping the fish back into the lake and smugly saying to them, "Welcome to my family."

Duke shouts, "Dude! I was gonna eat that!"

Lance sits down, cracks open a beer, puts his feet up and says with a satisfied smile, "Well, I wasn't. And I caught it. So, sue me."

Duke looks to Hank for support, but finds his dad smiling at Lance with respect.

★★★

Emmy opens the door to Art's house and chills run down her body as she finds him sitting on his couch, eyes red from a morning of tears. Art stands up to greet Emmy without his usual cowboy confidence and she asks with concern, "What happened?"

"Got a call this morning that Karl Torlakson is dead."

Emmy gasps. "How'd he die?"

Art forlornly shakes his head. "Police say he hung himself, but I don't know. Karl was a mess, but this just ain't his style. If he were goin' to kill himself he'd do it with drugs or booze. Hell, he was slowly doin' it already, but hangin'? I just don't know. He sure had his fair share of powerful enemies who could easily pull somethin' like this off."

"Do you want me to look into it? What if it's connected to the Altitude sabotage?"

"No. I don't want you gettin' near this and I called you over to tell you I'm takin' you off the whole case."

"What? I can't just walk away."

"You have to. It was a mistake for me to have ever even asked you to get involved in the first place. There are powerful groups out there that will let nothin' get in their way. My guess is Karl got caught up with one. If they get wind that you're sniffin' around, you'll be in grave danger."

"Okay, but I can at least advise you and look over all the information you get. There's no risk in that. You don't even have to pay me. I just want to help."

"Don't have to pay you? If anything, I'm goin' to pay you more for stayin' away."

Emmy rolls her eyes, pats Art on the back and asks, "So, what happens now with the board?"

"Hard to say, especially with things deadlocked. I think I'm goin' to ask Ronald to take Karl's spot."

"Ronald? Are you sure he's fit for a board?"

"I know, he's about two sandwiches short of a picnic, but he's got a good heart, he understands the culture of the company and he's friendly with both factions of the board. Plus, Karl came from sales, so it makes sense that he'd be replaced by another sales guy."

"I see your point. And he'd be in that swing vote position, so the secret buyer would have to make the pitch to Ronald, and when they do, we pounce."

"Precisely. Except there ain't no we. You leave the pouncin' to me."

★★★

Hank, Duke and Lance unload the fishing equipment from the truck as Emmy walks back to the house from Art's and asks, "How'd it go out there, boys?"

Duke grumpily says, "Your husband is a cooler."

Emmy looks confused. "What's a cooler?"

"He's bad luck. We didn't catch a single fish."

Lance smiles and says with satisfaction, "I call that good luck. And actually, one of us caught a fish, but I threw it back in."

"See! He's a saboteur," Duke says with an accusatory point at Lance as Emmy laughs out loud.

Hank laughs. "I'm not blamin' Lance, but that's the first time in the history of Benbrook Lake that we've come away empty handed."

"He's not allowed to fish with us anymore," Duke says, then grabs the ice chest and heads into the garage.

Lance whispers to Emmy with pride, "Mission Accomplished."

Chapter Fourteen

Day 110 of Pregnancy

Tree carries a large stack of plywood across the North Dallas High School auditorium stage. Nearby, a small construction crew is hard at work on the intricate Purple Sky set, which is being built on a rotating platform with the bakeshop and apartment on one side and the police station and city street on the other.

Principal Dwyer stands at the back of the auditorium, arms crossed with a look of amazement on his face at the impressive display of craftsmanship going on at the other end. Moments later, Ronald returns from the bathroom and says to Dwyer, "I hope you don't have to go anytime soon, because I just did some damage in the little boys' room. That ride is closed."

A look of pure disdain washes over Dwyer's face as he stares at Ronald. After a few moments of icy silence, Dwyer returns his gaze to the stage.

Not one for silence, Ronald leans in to Dwyer and says, "You must watch *The Breakfast Club* all the time."

Dwyer clenches his teeth as he considers how to deal with this odd little man and says coolly, "I've never seen it."

Ronald looks shocked and does a poor Mr. Vernon impression, "*What?! Well, you just bought yourself another Saturday, Mister!*"

"Today is Sunday," Dwyer replies, looking puzzled.

"It's from the movie. They had detention on Saturdays."

"Hm, that's not a bad idea. Wonder if I could pull that off," Dwyer muses aloud to himself.

Mistakenly thinking he and Dwyer are connecting, Ronald presses forward with the conversation. "Ah, so, you're more of an iron-fisted ruler like Mr. Vernon. Interesting. I would have pegged you more as the kindly neighbor-type like Mr. Feeny from *Boy Meets World*. Which, fun fact: Paul Gleason, who played Mr. Vernon in *Breakfast Club*, was also a guest star on *Boy Meets World*! How about that?"

Dwyer slowly turns his head and looks menacingly into Ronald's eyes. "If you say one more word, I'm going to tear up your rental contract."

Ronald nods in scared obedience, then whispers under his breath with a chuckle, "Classic Vernon."

★★★

Emmy unwraps her new maternity pillow with glee and tosses it on the bed. Lance looks in the mirror, examines some minor blemishes on his face and applies his face cream as Emmy lies down in bed, wraps her limbs around the plush, five feet long, snake-shaped pillow and says to Lance, "Spoon me!"

Lance laughs. "I don't think there's enough room on the bed for me now with your new pillow husband. Plus, we gotta get ready for Mass."

"I'm not up for going. Breakfast didn't sit well with me and I'm feeling super nauseous. Also, Duke has to work today, so you don't have any reason to leave."

"Actually, I do. Ronald just texted me that he left his meeting with Dwyer and wants to do lunch, so I told him I had to go to Mass. I never knew how handy this religion thing was. It's an excuse goldmine."

Emmy shakes her head and laughs. "You are such a holy man."

"Thank you," Lance replies with a smug smile.

"Seriously though, why do you need an excuse for Ronald? Just tell him you're spending quality time at home with your wife."

"Yeah, and then he'll barge in and try to cuddle us."

"I'll lock the doors."

"He'll climb through a window. Plus, your mom kind of spooked me with that whole danger thing. What if she's right?"

"I wouldn't worry about it."

"When we first started dating, you said your mom had a vision of me before you and I met and that her description matched me to a tee and you said that she has weirdly accurate visions like that a lot."

Emmy sighs. "Okay, yeah, I said that, but I highly doubt missing one Mass to spend an afternoon with your poor, pregnant wife is going to change things one way or another."

"Says the woman who isn't in grave danger," Lance replies as he pulls his suit from the closet.

Emmy laughs off his reference to danger. "Ohhh, I see, you just want to show off your fancy new suit."

"That is an outrageous accusation, Officer Ford. And also kind of true," Lance sheepishly admits and starts to buttons up his dress shirt. When he reaches the top button, a thought occurs to Lance and he turns to Emmy. "You think the danger your mom was talking about had to do with the Altitude case? I mean I was doing some heavy-duty undercover work and then the guy we did a sting on winds up dead. Coincidence? I think not."

"I think you've watched a few too many murder mysteries, but if your hypothesis is correct, then you are definitely staying home with me today because your services at my firm will no longer be needed. Art has taken me off the case."

"But it was just starting to get fun! And we need the money."

"He's still paying me. He actually gave me a raise."

Lance looks confused. "He's paying you more to stop working?"

"Yep."

"Does he have any jobs he wants to pay me to not do?"

"Yeah, in the wife-cuddling department."

"Fine, ten minutes and then I gotta go. Your mom wants to be extra early today."

"Half an hour. Take your car and meet them there."

Lance thinks it over for a moment then says, "Deal. I'll text her."

Emmy smiles victoriously as Lance grabs his phone and lies down next to her and her giant pillow.

Lance anxiously searches for a parking spot in the packed lot. At long last, he finds a spot in the very back, lodged between two large trucks. Despite his tiny car, he still struggles to squeeze his way out of the car and accidentally rubs his shoulder against the mud-caked exterior of the truck next to him and dirties his suit. He tries to pat the dirt off, but the spot remains. He silently curses as he opens the car door and squeezes his torso back inside, searching for a lint roller. At long last, he finds his lint roller, gets back out of the car and meticulously removes the dirt as a layer of sweat begins to accumulate over his entire body. Now dirt-free, Lance tosses the lint roller back in the car and begins the long, hot walk to the church. In the distance, he sees Hank's truck parked in one of the closest spots to the building and shakes his head in frustration.

By the time Lance enters the vestibule, he is dripping with sweat as an usher asks him to wait behind the various members of the procession, who line up in preparation for their entrance. Moments later, Ronald enters the vestibule and says, "Fancy meeting you here!"

Lance silently laments his decision to use Mass as his excuse and manages to force a smile and give Ronald a friendly shush. Ronald whispers, "Sorry," then stifles a giggle. After composing himself he adds in a whisper, "Look at that, I'm in a Catholic church ten seconds and I'm already guilty."

Lance uses his hand to wipe his sweaty forehead as Ronald looks at him with concern, hands him a handkerchief and asks, "You okay?"

"My parking spot was in Houston. By the time I walked here I was drenched."

Ronald laughs. "Houston. That's a good line. Can I use that?"

"It's not that good, but you can have it. By the way, this is the first time I've ever seen you not sweat. Where did you park?"

"I actually took an Über. I figured I'd find you eventually and you could give me a ride home," Ronald whispers to a thoroughly perplexed Lance.

Lance finishes wiping down his face as Ronald whispers, "I only blew my nose into that one three times."

A look of disgust comes over Lance's face as Ronald laughs out loud and immediately covers his mouth to silence the laugh. Lance tosses the handkerchief back at Ronald who whispers, "I'm kidding. Just an old joke from my Catholic school days."

"You grew up Catholic?"

"No, but a lot of big stars in Hollywood are lapsed Catholics, so I'm workshopping it as a back-story."

"Of course, you are," Lance says as the choir begins to sing the entrance hymn and the procession makes its way into the church. Ronald attempts to join the procession, but an usher intervenes and guides him and Lance to an open spot in the back corner of the packed church with a large pillar obstructing half of Lance's view.

At the conclusion of the opening hymn and prayers, the congregation sits down for the first reading and Ronald whispers to Lance, "What kind of fun does a priest have?"

Lance sighs. "What?"

"Nun," Ronald whispers and stifles a giggle as Lance mirthlessly buries his head in his hands.

Ronald leans in. "How do you get rid of a nun's hiccups?"

Lance glares at Ronald and whispers, "If you finish that joke, I'm quitting the play and keeping your money."

"But it's a really good one!" Ronald pleads as Lance continues his glare. After a moment's consideration, Ronald shakes his head in defeat and whispers, "Your loss."

Lance attempts to turn his attention back to the reading, but his body sweat is now sticky and dry from the powerful air-conditioning and a fierce itch begins to build on the back of his neck. He scratches it, but the itch moves down below his shirt collar and he struggles to reach it.

Ronald leans in to the elderly woman next to him and points at Lance. "Who invited Mr. Itchy-Pants?"

★★★

The country club gym is bustling with activity as Duke assists Judith on her final bench press rep and guides the barbell into its holder, taking every opportunity to glance at her tight, skimpy outfit. Judith lies for a moment on the bench, takes a deep breath and stands up, sweat glistening on her forehead from the long, private workout and says, "Wow, you are kicking my butt, Duke."

"Whoa, I would never kick that work of art," Duke replies with a wink as he motions to her rear end.

Judith stuffs down the urge to snap at Duke and flirtatiously replies, "Watch it, Mister."

"Sorry, I know, I promised I'd be professional. You up for another set of curls?"

"No, I'm beat. I think I'll just do a couple more miles on the elliptical then head home," Judith says as she walks over to a nearby chair and sits down to hydrate.

"Well, if you change your mind, I'll be workin' my glamour muscles in the free weight room," Duke says, stretching his arms and torso in an attempt to show off said glamour muscles. He adds, "Now, I like to end every session by discussing your emotional health. Anything stressing you out?"

Judith looks at Duke with eyebrows raised and says, "Wow, that's shockingly enlightened."

"I like to take a holistic approach to my clients."

"Well, it's a pleasure to meet you, sensitive Duke. Let's see… What is stressing me out? Memorizing all my lines in the play is somewhat stressful. And Ronald has been really overwhelmed with work and everything he has to do for the play so that hasn't helped, especially in the aftermath of that design leak. I really hope Emmy can find out who was responsible for that and bring them to justice. It has created so much extra work for my hubby," Judith says with fake concern. She glances at a sympathetic Duke and seizing her opportunity to mine for more info, innocently asks, "You don't happen to have any more news on Emmy's investigation, do you? I promise I won't tell a soul. I just need to know something is being done."

Duke ponders for a moment then says, "I'm sorry to say, I don't think she's got much. Every time I see her workin' on stuff, she looks frustrated. And I don't think it's just a pregnancy hormone thing. I think she's stumped. The leaker is free."

Judith quells her internal joy at this news, feigns disappointment and says, "That's too bad."

"Yeah, sometimes the good guys just don't win. Is there anything else you wanted to get off your chest?"

Judith smiles at Duke, "No, you know, I feel so much better after our chat. Thank you for that, Duke. You truly are a wonderful trainer."

"I'm wonderful at a lot of things..." Duke suavely replies.

"And now I'm queasy."

"I meant wonderful at a lot of things related to fitness, mental health and friendship," Duke plaintively replies as Judith stands up, puts on her headphones and walks away. Duke shakes his head as he watches her leave and says under his breath, "Man, she is tough. What's Ronald's secret?"

At the conclusion of Mass, as parishioners begin to file out, Lance sits in silence and stares at the pillar in front of him, shell-shocked from the socially-harrowing hour he spent with Ronald, who taps Lance on the shoulder and says, "Come on, the line outside to talk to the priest is getting really long and I want to run some jokes by him."

Lance musters up his last bit of patience and asks, "Are you sure that's a good idea?"

"Of course! I think I can help him. Let's be honest, we didn't hear a whole lot of laughs during his sermon."

"He was talking about the death of his father."

"Listen, the greats can be funny no matter the topic. Have you not seen Carrot Top? You know what, I don't have time to explain stand-up comedy to you, I need to get in that line, so just find me out there when you're done with... Whatever it is you're doing here," Ronald replies impatiently and rushes out of the church as Lupita and Hank approach Lance who looks apologetically at them.

"Lance, you made it! We were worried you got lost," Hank says with a laugh.

"I'm sorry, I was late. Had a few mishaps."

Lupita smiles with sympathy. "No need to apologize, I'm proud of you."

"You are?"

"Of course," she says, motioning to Ronald in line as she continues, "you brought someone with you, eso es evangelismo."

Lance laughs. "No, no, no. I'm not taking the blame if that guy joins. He only came so he could force me into having lunch with him."

Hank chuckles. "Hey, we all have our reasons. I only came so I don't have to sleep on the couch."

"That is not funny, Hank," Lupita says with a glare.

"I'm kidding!" Hank says to Lupita then secretly winks at Lance as they make their way out of the church. Hank looks back at the still-sitting Lance and says, "You comin'?"

"I'll see you guys back at home. Going to just enjoy the quiet while I can."

After a few minutes of silence, Lance's solace is interrupted as Ronald rushes up to him and says guiltily, "I'm so sorry, but I'm going to have to take a rain check on lunch. I just saw Art and he asked if I was free for lunch to go over some work stuff and I just can't turn down the boss. Really, really sorry."

Lance feigns disappointment. "Dang, well I understand, work comes first."

"Thanks, Man. Also, you were right about the priest jokes. He didn't love my material, so I don't think I'll be coming around here again anytime soon," Ronald says with a shrug, then rushes out of the church leaving Lance blissfully alone.

Lance laughs to himself, looks up to the Heavens and says, "Maybe you are listening."

★★★

Art and Ronald sit across from each other at a large table in the elegantly decorated outdoor patio of Muchacho's Tex Mex as Ronald details the impressive stage set that Tree is building and mentions that he met Principal Dwyer.

Art looks concerned at the mention of Dwyer. "Listen, if Dwyer gives you a hard time, just let me know and I'll set him straight."

"You are very kind, but I don't think that will be necessary. We really hit it off. He was diggin' all my movie references."

"He was?" Art asks in total surprise.

"Big time. I could feel a real friendship brewing."

"You sure that was Principal Dwyer?"

"Yes sir! I know Lance struggled to connect with him, but he's one of those genius artist types, they don't really know how to talk to the suits. I have a way with people... So, what'd you want to talk about?"

"Well, first off, I'm assuming you heard about Karl Torlakson..."

Ronald grows somber and says, "Yeah, I did. Tragic."

"It was. I'm still strugglin', but life must go on. That's what I wanted to discuss with you. I know it's early, but when the time comes, I'd like to nominate you to replace him on the board. I know typically we don't put current employees on the board, but you and Karl have similar backgrounds, you're friendly with all the members and I just think it would be a great fit."

Ronald stares for a moment then says, "Wow, I mean, I'm absolutely honored, but I just don't know if I can add any more to my plate."

"I know, but hear me out. By the time you're officially added to the board, this whole leak thing will be ancient history and the play will have already been done."

"True," Ronald says. He ponders for a moment before adding, "But I really think we got a good shot at getting picked up by one of the big producers on Broadway. Maybe they'll even turn it into a movie! So, as much as I'd love to do it and am beyond appreciative that you thought of me, I really need to keep my options open long term."

Art smiles at Ronald like a Dad whose un-athletic son just told him he plans to play in the NBA. "I understand. We can always put an opt-out clause in your contract should any lucrative entertainment deals come your way. Just think it over."

Chapter Fifteen

Day 115 of Pregnancy

L ance and Emmy stare intently at the ultrasound screen as Dr. Bethany Chung, a bright-eyed obstetrician in her late thirties, guides the ultrasound wand over Emmy's belly and says, "I obviously can't confirm one hundred percent, but I think I see a little wee wee. I would say it's likely you have a little boy in there."

Lance pumps his fist with excitement and squeezes Emmy's hand.

Dr. Chung laughs and says to Lance, "That's what you were hoping for, I see."

"Yup. Don't get me wrong, I want a girl too, but I want the boy first so I can train him to beat up anyone who bullies our little girl."

Emmy interjects, "Or he could end up terrorizing her like Duke did to me."

Dr. Chung laughs as she concludes the ultrasound and brings the appointment to a close. Just when Dr. Chung is about to leave the room, Emmy says, "By the way, if you're free Saturday, June twenty-second, you should come see Lance's play! He wrote it and stars in it!"

Lance nervously runs his hands through his hair. "Oh no, you really don't have to. It might not be that good."

Emmy furrows her brow and says to Lance, "What do you mean? You said the cast was great and the picture you showed me of Tree's set looked phenomenal."

"Yeah, but what if it's bad. What if the whole thing is a failure? Then for the next five months it's going to be awkward every time we have an appointment," Lance says to Emmy. He turns to Dr. Chung and diplomatically says, "It's okay if you'd rather not come."

"No, I would love to come. My husband is actually one of the entertainment writers for the Dallas Morning News. I'm sure he'd be happy to give you guys a write-up before and after."

Lance perks up. "Really? That would be awesome! Thank you so much."

"My pleasure! Just email me the details and we'll see you guys on the twenty-second," Dr. Chung replies with a "thumbs up" and exits the room as Lance stares in shock at Emmy.

"What just happened?"

"I think I'm your new publicist," Emmy says with pride as she takes off the medical gown and begins to put on her clothes back on.

"You sure are. That would be huge if he gives us a plug beforehand. A full theater can mask a lot of blemishes. Although I think I may have made a casting mistake…"

"Which one?"

"You know that Willie Nelson impersonator I told you about?"

"Yeah, where does Ronald find these people?"

"He's an enigma. Anyway, I cast Willie for the role of a middle-aged woman as a prank on Ronald because I thought no one would come and it would be hilarious to see Ronald have to act like Willie Nelson is his wife. But since the play itself is serious and a serious journalist coming, I think I may look like a directorial buffoon with such a cartoonish choice."

"Oh, you'll be fine. I mean, Willie Nelson has long hair, so as long as he shaves his beard and can do a convincing voice, no one will even notice."

"He won't shave the beard. He needs it for his music gigs. And I'm pretty sure your Dad would have a more convincing falsetto."

"Yikes. Can't you just cast someone else?"

"I guess, but we're already three weeks away and casting takes time. Plus, he's really excited about playing a woman and I need to keep him happy because he's perfect as the postman."

"He's playing two parts?!"

"Yeah, again, I did it as a joke, when I thought no one would see it and then my wife had to go and invite a legit journalist," Lance replies with a playful defensiveness.

"Don't hate me just because I'm better at my publicist job than you are at your directing job."

Lance gives her a smug smile, takes a deep breath and says, "You know what, it's okay, in the midst of a dark, serious murder mystery, we are going to have a bearded lady on that stage and at best, the audience loves it, at worst, I'm seen as an edgy iconoclast imported from the progressive land of exotic San Francisco."

"Or it will undermine the entire mood and narrative of the play, drawing attention away from your incredible writing and the carefully cultivated performances of your actors, leaving the audience confused and underwhelmed."

"Thank you for that very eloquent vote of confidence."

"Just keepin' it real."

Lance pensively nods. "I'll see what I can do."

★★★

Ronald sings the chorus to George Benson's "On Broadway," as he dances down the dimly-lit hotel hallway and stops in front of Chet, who looks at Ronald with disdain and opens the hotel room door.

"Thanks, Doll-face," Ronald says in his best New York accent and stuffs a one-dollar bill in Chet's breast pocket before walking into the darkness.

Chet looks down at the single poking out of his jacket, fights the urge to punch Ronald and closes the door.

Ronald stands in silence and shields his eyes from the impending spotlight blast. After a few moments, the cowboy greets him without turning on the spotlight. "What day is it, Ronald?"

Ronald pulls out his phone and looks down at it. "Let's see, it is Friday, May 31st in the year of our Lord, 2019."

"The year of our Lord?"

"Sorry, that's how we were taught to say it back in my Catholic school days. Old habits die hard!"

"I see. So, it ain't Tuesday?"

Ronald suddenly grows serious and says with a guilty sigh, "No."

"Hm. And what day did Judith tell you to be here?"

"Tuesday."

"That was three days ago. You stood me up. And you know what happens when I get stood up? I start to worry. And you know what happens when I start to worry?"

"You binge eat?"

The spotlight suddenly turns on and blasts the eyes of an unprepared Ronald with blinding light. Ronald winces in pain and shouts, "Oh, come on! That was funny!"

"When I worry, I suddenly feel like I have to protect myself. Which can be very bad for the person I'm worried about."

"Okay, I'll be totally honest, I have been so damn busy and I genuinely forgot. Plus, you don't have a cell phone and Chet won't give me his number, but even if he did, this place is like a black hole for cell reception. There are doomsday bunkers that get a better signal."

"Actually, my doomsday bunker gets perfect reception."

"Okay, that was a good one. Credit where credit is due. But seriously, I have been extremely busy and I am so sorry that I stood you up."

The cowboy laughs with condescension. "Judith told me about your little play."

Chills run down Ronald's body as he asks with trepidation, "She told you about it?"

"She did. And she's giving me free tickets. Is that okay?"

"Of course... The more the merrier..." Ronald says with a gulp of nervous air. He takes a breath and asks hopefully, "Is that all you wanted to see me about?"

"No. We need to talk about Art. I understand you don't want to accept that man's very generous offer."

"Yeah, I would, but again, I just have too much on my plate to join the board."

"Interesting. And what if I were to take away that full plate and replace it with a gun to your head? Would that help matters?"

Ronald shudders and says with a trembling jaw. "Listen, I thought we agreed that after I did the leak, I was free."

The cowboy cackles. "We didn't agree to a damn thing, Boy. The oath is for life. So, you're goin' to be a good soldier. You're goin' to join the board and you're goin' to sell Altitude. Got it?"

Ronald clenches his teeth and says, "Got it."

Evening twilight sets in as Ronald and Judith hold hands and walk through the North Dallas High parking lot on their way to rehearsals. Judith looks over at Ronald's grumpy face and says sympathetically, "I'm sorry, Honey, but he was going to find out one way or another."

"I know, but if it were his goons telling him about the play, I doubt he goes. But when the prettiest woman in Texas tells him? Of course, he's going to show up. How am I supposed to stay in the zone when that guy is watching?"

"Come on, just think positive. Tell yourself he's going to love the play. Plus, he's one of the richest men in America and Lucid owns a media company, so after he sees how great the play is, he could be inspired to turn it into a movie. It would be everything you've ever wanted!"

"He'd be the perfect producer," Ronald says sarcastically before doing an impression of the cowboy, "'Ronald, you're over budget, I'm goin' to have to kill you. Ronald, you flubbed that line, I'm goin' to have to kill you. Ronald, you're too damn handsome on screen, I'm goin' to have to kill you.'"

"You really mean to tell me that if he offered you a movie deal, you'd turn it down? You'd say no to millions of dollars and a career in film?"

Ronald thinks it over for a moment and says, "Okay, maybe that would be hard to turn down. But I would at least demand a clause in the contract that says he's not allowed to kill me."

Judith shakes her head and says with a chuckle, "You are so principled."

Inside the auditorium, Tree turns on the hydraulic spinning stage and shows it to Lance, who watches in awe and says, "That is exactly like my old SF Playhouse stage! How did you build it so quickly?"

Tree smiles with pride. "It's amazing what construction workers can do when you offer to double their pay for finishing early."

Lance laughs. "Well, it's incredible and I am so stoked that we get to rehearse here now."

Emmy, Lupita and Hank sit at their sparkling dining room table with Art, who packs up his poker chips after a lively game of Texas Hold 'Em. As Art stands up and bids them goodbye, Hank continues to gloat about his dominance and Emmy offers to walk Art out. When they reach the front door, Art says to Emmy, "Ronald accepted my offer. Once we hammer out the details and confirm everything is a go with the board, we'll have our guy."

Emmy offers a relieved smile. "Perfect. We need something because your team is giving me absolutely nothing to go on leak-wise."

Art sighs. "Yeah, unfortunately I think that leaker is goin' to get off scot free on that one."

"It kills me that I couldn't do more. And now I'm in the same boat with this Ronald thing. I know you'd rather lose the company than see me get hurt, but there are things I know I can do that will not put me in harm's way. I promise."

Art bites his lip and replies, "I'm listenin'…"

"Okay, so all I ask is tomorrow night, when Ronald and all them are rehearsing, I drive over to North Dallas High and put a tracking device on his car. I'll buy one that'll allow me to track where he goes from the safety of my own home. You know the people behind all this garbage aren't stupid enough to try and flip him by e-mail or phone. They'll do it face to face. So, if I see any suspicious trips, I will immediately send you an alert and you and/or your guys can rush over and see what he's up to. Deal?"

Art takes a deep breath, stares up at the ceiling for a moment then turns back to Emmy and nods.

Emmy's face lights up. "Really? You'll let me?"

"Yeahhh, I will. I know you pretty darn well and if I say no, you'll just end up goin' rogue and doin' it all yourself without tellin' me. At least this way when everything goes down, you'll be stayin' home."

Emmy hugs Art with gratitude and says, "Definitely. I'll be home safe and sound. Time to trap us some snakes."

★★★

Lance and Ronald stroll along the walls of the auditorium awaiting the arrival of the cast as Judith quietly practices her lines on stage and Tree continues to put the finishing touches on the bakeshop set.

"So, I have some big news," Lance says to Ronald.

"You're getting a sex-change."

"What? No. I meant about the play. Why would you think I'm getting a sex-change?"

"I don't know, for the publicity? I just read a blog about how to gain followers on social media and one of the things they said is documenting a gender transition is super effective, so I thought maybe you had read the same thing."

"No, I didn't. And I'm not. So, back on Planet Earth, thanks to Emmy, the Dallas Morning News is not only going to promote our play, but one of their top writers will be in attendance and covering it," Lance says triumphantly as Ronald stares in wide-eyed silence.

"Are you okay?" Lance asks with concern.

Ronald suddenly breaks his stunned silence with a scream, "We're going to be famous!"

Judith shushes Ronald from across the auditorium and shouts, "Babe, I'm trying to rehearse!"

"Sorry, Honey!" Ronald meekly replies. He lowers his voice and says to Lance, "This is incredible! How did she do it?"

"She told our obstetrician about the play and it just so happened that her husband is some big time entertainment writer for the paper. But, we need to talk about something. Willie can't play your wife. Not with the kind of press we'll be getting."

Ronald breathes a sigh of relief. "I couldn't agree more. Honestly, I was shocked you wanted him in that role. I figured, you're the professional, and if I have to kiss a bearded lady to bring your vision to life, I'll do it, but I'd rather keep these lips for the ladies or Matt Damon. So, whom are we going to cast as my wife? I can see if Judith has any model-friends that are available…"

"Actually, I was thinking I could just re-write the play so that the bakeshop murder that Jack and I are investigating was a double-homicide and she was the second casualty. I think it'll be easier to explain that to Willie than coming up with a reason for firing him and casting someone else. We can't risk losing him as our postman."

"Good point, he definitely seemed excited to play a woman… Although, who wouldn't want to be my wife, am I right?" Ronald says with a grunt as he playfully elbows Lance.

Chapter Sixteen

Day 116 of Pregnancy

E mmy pins the latest ultrasound pictures to the wall above her home office desk as Lance paces around the room, pen in one hand, *Purple Sky* script in the other, silently mouthing dialogue and making notes. She looks over at him and says, "Can I interrupt for just a second?"

Lance continues to make notes without responding; then looks up at her as though he just awoke from a dream and replies with a glance at the pictures, "They look perfect," then turns his attention back to the script.

On the other side of Emmy's closed office door, Duke is just about to give up on his daily eavesdropping when he overhears Emmy say to Lance, "It's not about the pictures. It's about the Altitude case."

Duke's eyes go wide with anticipation as he strains to hear every word. Back in the room, Lance suddenly closes the script and replies with excitement, "We're back in business?"

"Oh, so that's what it takes for you to pay attention to your poor pregnant wife?"

"I'm sorry, I just have been struggling to find a way to kill Ronald's wife."

In the hallway, a look of confused horror goes over Duke's face.

"Judith's acting is that bad?" Emmy replies.

"Very funny. No, I am taking the advice of my poor pregnant wife and eliminating the need for Willie Nelson to dress in drag by making her a casualty in the bakeshop murder. But what's going on with the case?"

Duke breathes a sigh of relief and shakes his head in embarrassment for momentarily thinking Lance might be a murderer.

Emmy sits down in her office chair and lowers her voice. "Well, Ronald is going to replace Karl Torlakson on the board, and I know you're going to say, 'What're they nuts?' No, they are not, and Art has good reasons for choosing him. Now, the plan is to track Ronald so that when the shysters try to bring him in and turn him to the dark side, we can smoke 'em out."

"We? You're not smoking anyone or anything, Miss. I'll take care of the bad guys," Lance says with a flex.

"Sorry, Captain America. Neither of us will be involved in the smoking portion of the plan. Art and his team will take care of that."

"Yeah, that's probably for the best. I'm really only trained in stage-fighting."

"There won't be any fighting. There may not even be any talking. This is just so Art can find out who he's competing with."

Duke's eavesdropping is interrupted by the sound of Lupita walking up the stairs leading to the hallway. He mouths a curse word before silently tiptoeing away to his bedroom.

Emmy pauses at the sound of footsteps on the stairs and stays silent until she hears her mom close the door to the master bedroom, then continues, "So, here's the plan, tonight while y'all are rehearsing, I am going to put the tracker on Ronald's truck. I will let you know when I arrive and when I leave and I need you to text me if anyone leaves the building so I can hide. Got it?"

Lance smiles with excitement as he imitates the theme music to *Mission Impossible*.

Emmy rolls her eyes. "This is serious. If we screw up it'll jeopardize the entire plan."

"Sorry. Yes. I got it," Lance replies with a serious salute. Moments later the excitement busts out again and he says in a deep, official voice, "Your mission, should you choose accept it…"

Emmy sighs as Lance once again does the *Mission Impossible* theme.

The cast stands in a circle on stage as Lance leads them in their final vocal warm-up. After transitioning into a series of standing stretches, the cast sits down and Lance demonstrates a series of yoga poses. As everyone makes an attempt at the fish pose, Lance calmly says, "Alright, improv time. I want everyone to imagine you are a fish. Think about what fish you are. Think about where you are. Feel yourself swimming through the cool, crisp water of a rushing river or gliding through the warm water of a tropical bay. Live in that for a moment and then feel free to tell your fellow fish what kind of fish you are…"

Predictably, Ronald is the first to speak. "I am Nemo, the most beloved clown fish in the world!"

Lance shakes his head. "Of course, you are."

Judith continues the cinematic theme. "I'm Jaws, stalking my prey through the ocean, ready to chomp a bite out of every boat in my path."

Before Lance can comment on the scary nature of Judith's vision, Tree says, "I am Willy, ready to be freed by my little human friend!"

Lance replies, "Not that I don't love the movie references, but you can just be a regular fish…"

Knucks cockily says, "I'm a fish that gets all the broads whenever I want—"

Lance interrupts, "Okayyy, once again, warm-ups are a misogyny-free zone, Knucks."

"Spoken like a true Beta Fish," Knucks replies as Brent and Rob laugh in support.

"You know what, let's just get going on the rehearsal. Everyone up," Lance says as the class gingerly rises from the floor. He continues, "Before we begin our run-through, I just wanted to let you guys know there's been a slight change to the script. I've printed out new copies for everyone."

Lance nods at Ronald who opens a nearby cardboard box, pulls out a stack of scripts and begins to hand them out. Lance looks down at his phone and reads a text from Emmy informing him that she has arrived at the parking lot. Lance puts his phone back in his pocket and says, "I'm sorry if you've already marked up your current script. It would be too difficult to manually change the ones you already have, so I'll give you guys some time to read through the new version and copy down your previous notes. Once everyone has read it, we'll discuss the changes."

In the outside lot, Emmy parks her S.U.V. next to Ronald's truck and preps the tracking device. She runs a few tests, scans the parking lot for signs of life and exits the Emmy-mobile. She swiftly examines the contours of the truck and chooses the front plastic bumper as her ideal location for the tracker.

Inside, Lance watches with trepidation as Willie reads through the script, his expression growing darker with every page. Ronald walks over to Lance and whispers, "He doesn't look happy. Say something, Boss."

Lance thinks for a moment before addressing the cast. "The major change I think you guys will notice is the killing of the bakeshop owner's wife. We felt like making it a double-murder would increase the stakes of the investigation and then Willie, you don't have to worry about playing multiple characters; that's a lot to ask. Now you can focus fully on the juicy postman role."

Willie shakes his head in anger and storms out of the auditorium. Lance and the cast stare in awkward silence for a moment; then Lance remembers Emmy's presence outside and reaches in his pocket to text her a warning.

Back outside, Emmy lies on the pavement and reaches into the front bumper to attach the tracker as her phone buzzes with Lance's message. She bites her lip in frustration, reads the text and swiftly slides out from under the truck before rushing into the backseat of the Emmy-mobile. She slowly raises her head and watches from behind the black, tinted windows as Willie walks to the parking lot, pulls out an expensive Cuban cigar, lights it up and begins to smoke it with a look of sheer pleasure.

Emmy whispers to herself in frustration, "Really? A cigar? This is going to take forever."

Willie smokes the cigar for what feels like an hour to Emmy, but in actuality is no more than ten minutes, then flicks the partially smoked cigar onto the ground, snuffs it out with his boot and suddenly starts to laugh like a man possessed. Emmy watches with disturbed confusion as Willie regains his composure, puts on a look of hurt anger and begins his walk back to the auditorium.

"What the heck was that?" Emmy says to herself before scanning the parking lot and exiting the backseat to resume her work.

The cast continues to mark up their scripts when Willie returns to the auditorium, the air still thick with awkward tension as he walks to the back row and sits down.

Ronald nudges a reluctant Lance to go talk to the glum-looking Willie and he obliges, but forces Ronald to come with him.

Ronald stands in the aisle and watches Lance sit down next to Willie and say, "I'm really sorry, Willie. I know you wanted to nail that role, but it just seemed like the right thing to do. And you are spectacular as the postman. Truly. Better than the professional actor who played him back in San Francisco."

Ronald interjects, "I fought him hard on this one, but Lance just wouldn't budge." Lance glares at Ronald, who continues, "And after thinking long and hard, I realized that as much as I wanted you to be my wife, it really is better this way. We'll even let you improvise a monologue about the perils of mail carrying in the second act."

Lance stares in disbelief at Ronald's unsanctioned monologue and is about to correct him when Willie begins to softly sing, "Blue Eyes Crying in the Rain."

Ronald closes his eyes and sways to the song. Lance listens patiently, but grows increasingly uncomfortable as it becomes clear that Willie is going to sing the entire song.

Willie concludes and Ronald, Lance and the rest of the class applaud dutifully. Willie nods with gratitude, then turns to Lance and says, "Thank you for the explanation. I respect your decision and I look forward to my monologue."

Lance fights the urge to shut down the monologue idea and says with a gulp, "As do I." He stands up and walks with Ronald back to the stage.

Ronald leans in and whispers, "Am I a genius or what?"

Lance stares stone-faced at Ronald and says, "I would go with the 'or what.'"

"Come on! Everyone loves postal worker stories! Rain, sleet, snow, all that good stuff."

"Yes, who can forget the iconic scene in *L.A. Confidential* when, in the midst of the investigation, the local barber delivers a lengthy monologue about the fineries of cutting hair."

"I don't remember that scene."

"Of course you don't, because if the director included it, he would be fired."

"Was it a deleted scene? Because I don't think my copy has the special features so I'll need to borrow yours."

Lance gives up on the conversation as his phone buzzes with a text from Emmy that reads: "Job is done. Also, that Willie Nelson guy might be insane. Just an F.Y.I. Love you!"

Chapter Seventeen

Day 117 of Pregnancy

Emmy wakes up and groggily feels around the empty bed in search of Lance. She gingerly pulls herself up, puts on her slippers and exits the bedroom. Emmy wipes the sleep from her eyes and pads into the living room where Lance is in the middle of a long yoga session and Lupita is sitting beside him, praying the Rosary. Emmy stares in sleepy confusion and says, "I don't know how I feel about you two being such good friends."

Lance chuckles as he slides down from his shoulder stand, gets up and kisses Emmy good morning. "How'd you sleep, Babe?"

"Wait, no. First off, how are you awake before me? And what are you and my mom doing?"

Lance replies innocently, "Exactly what it looks like. I'm doing yoga and she's educating me on the finer points of the Rosary. Well, she was, now she's actually doing it, so maybe keep your voice down." He lowers his voice, pulls Rosary beads from his pocket and continues, "You know, I always thought these were just necklaces that scary Latin men wore, but apparently it's a whole big thing. Your mom gave me the lowdown. Also, you should Google 'Our Lady of Guadalupe Tilma' and read up on it. The history of that thing will blow your mind."

"Lance, I'm half-Salvadorian, you really think I don't know the history of the tilma?"

"Someone woke up on the wrong side of the maternity pillow."

"I'm sorry?"

"Yeah, I wanted that one back as soon as it came out."

Emmy hits Lance with a playful jab to the arm and heads to the kitchen as Lance walks over to Lupita and continues his stretching.

Art and Jack stand outside the church passing out bulletins in fulfillment of their bi-weekly greeter duties at the noon Mass. During a lull in entrants, Jack turns to Art and says, "I know you don't like the sentimental stuff, but I just have to say, I really appreciate how you've been sticking up for me with the board. Especially adding Ronald. Having a friend like him in that group is going to be so huge for me. Although, I still wonder if I have what it takes to fill your shoes. How many times in history has the son or son-in-law of the great business leader wrecked the company after taking over?"

Art stares pensively off into the distance as only a grizzled Texan can, then turns to Jack and replies, "Character."

"Character?"

"That's right. Character. Long as you continue to be a man of character, I ain't worried. That fancy M.B.A. of yours, the success you've had with Altitude, none of that factored into my decision. I chose you because you treat the folks who clean our planes the same way you treat the board. I could find any number of brilliant businessmen to continue to grow the company, but I don't know them like I know you. Stay true to who are and you'll be just fine."

Jack nods with gratitude and looks across the courtyard at an approaching Emmy, Lupita and Hank, followed by Lance, who trails behind them with a look of paranoia. Emmy turns back to Lance and asks, "What are you doing?"

Lance lowers his voice. "I'm making sure Ronald isn't here."

"You said he just came last Sunday to force you into lunch…"

"Yeah, except we didn't have lunch. He said we'd do a rain check. What if he's coming to cash that check today?"

"Then just have lunch with him."

"It's not lunch I'm worried about. It's Mass. You have no idea what I went through."

"Oh, he couldn't have been that bad."

"It was like sharing a pew with a rabid monkey. If that rabid monkey had memorized four hundred horrible Catholic street jokes."

Emmy laughs him off as they reach Art and Jack. Emmy leans in to give Art a kiss on the cheek and whispers, "The tracker is in place."

Art gives her a knowing wink, hands her a bulletin and says with a smile, "Enjoy Mass now, ya hear?"

★★★

Duke wears punch-mitts on both hands and holds them out to Judith, who stares with intensity at her target and readies her boxing-gloved hands.

"Okay, let's see what you got," Duke says with a wry smile as Judith unleashes a flurry of powerful, precise punch combinations on Duke's mitts.

"Damn? Where'd you learn to punch like that? Is there a beauty queen fight club I don't know about?"

Judith laughs. "Something like that. Now, can we keep training or are you scared I'm going to bust your hands?"

"Oh, really? That's how you want to do this?" Duke replies, then preps his mitts for another round, this time displaying his own boxing prowess by lightly jabbing her in the stomach or head each time she leaves an opening.

At the end of the workout, Judith pats Duke on the shoulder and says, "You're the first trainer I've found who can keep up with me. I used to have to go to boxing gyms for a good session, but I guess I won't have to now."

Duke smiles with pride and says, "Well, I'm the gift that keeps on giving, because I have some great news on the Altitude investigation."

Judith's eyes light up as she gently rubs his arm. "Tell me!"

"Well, I happened to overhear Emmy say that they think the guys that did the leak are trying to get the company and will probably try to meet up with Ronald once he's on the board to flip him. So, the plan is, Art's crew is going to secretly follow Ronald around so they can find out who the bad guys are."

"No way! That's such a great plan! Is Emmy going to be the one following Ronald?"

"No. I heard her say she wasn't going to be involved and I had to run before I could hear the details of the plan, so I don't know who will be doing the following or how they're going to do it, but I figured you'd be pretty stoked to hear that there is a plan and that Ronald is the key to cracking the case!"

Judith does her best lying smile and says wistfully, "My hero."

"Now, when you say hero, do you mean me or Ronald?"

"Ronald," Judith replies matter-of-factly.

Duke hides his disappointment. "Of course. I was just joking around. Obviously, it would be Ronald."

"Thank you for that information though, Duke. I feel much better now," Judith says with a calm smile, then walks off in the direction of the women's locker room.

Duke's eyes follow Judith and he says under his breath, "Man, oh man, I hate to see her go, but I love to watch her leave."

Chapter Eighteen

Day 118 of Pregnancy

J udith wears large, black Prada sunglasses as she stands confidently in the pitch-black hotel room. The spotlight turns on and Judith unflinchingly says, "Why didn't I wear these sooner?"

The cowboy cackles. "Because you're stubborn as a mule. The sunglasses are an admission of defeat and you ain't a woman who admits defeat easily."

"And when I wear sunglasses outside, is that admitting defeat?"

"You better believe it. I would never let Helios have the satisfaction of seeing me in sunglasses."

"Helios?"

"The Greek god of the Sun," he replies as though she had just asked what two plus two equals.

"I thought that was Apollo…"

"Helios was the original. He carried the sun up to the sky. Apollo just glommed on when it was convenient," the cowboy says with an irrational level of antipathy towards Apollo.

"Got it. Well, I have news. They're now following Ronald," Judith says with a note of caution.

"They? Who's they, Darlin'?"

"I don't know. I'm assuming it would be Art's Keystone Cops inside Altitude. Art seems to think that you'll reach out to Ronald once he's on the board and they'll finally find out who's been behind everything. But it's an easy fix. Ronald will stay away and I'll relay any messages to him that you need."

The cowboy laughs. "That's the best Art can do? Sad. Now, to the important stuff, have you memorized your lines?"

Judith chuckles. "I have indeed. It's honestly a great play. Really is too bad that Lance has to die; he's talented. I mean, seriously, if I were running your media company, I'd hire him to write some films."

"Better yet, after he's dead, we can just buy the rights to whatever he's already written. He'll be a legend. And if Jack's bullet isn't fatal, we'll sign Lance to a contract and put him on all the morning shows. They'll eat the murder attempt angle right up."

Judith nods in approval. "It's a win-win."

"Now, let's go back a sec. You said 'if you were running my media company.' Would you like to run it?"

"Of course. Once Ronald is out of the way, it would be a dream. I just can't fathom working in Hollywood with him around."

"Oh, definitely. He'd be out of the picture for sure. But I do think that's the right place for you. They got some real big snakes out there, but you're a cobra if I've ever seen one. Finish this job, and you'll get a first-class ticket to Hollywood, courtesy of Altitude Airlines."

★★★

"Topeka Topeka Topeka!" Lance says in a rapid falsetto as he stands in the middle of the cast circle on stage. He deepens his voice and continues the vocal warm-up as they attempt to repeat after him with mixed results, "Lo Lay Lee Lie Low Lew Lo Lay Lee Lie Low Lew! Can't you, don't you, won't you, can't you, don't you, won't you, can't you, don't you, won't you!"

The back doors to the auditorium open with a squeak. Lance looks over and sighs at the sight of Mr. and Mrs. Dwyer entering the auditorium, walking down the main aisle and taking seats in the third row. Ronald offers a friendly wave to Dwyer, who stares back with contempt.

"Alright, guys we're going to jump right into a full run-through of the play, top to bottom, so do whatever you need to do to get set. We have to be fully off-book by this weekend, so if you want to give it a go without your script, do so and if you forget your line, just yell 'line' and someone will feed it to you. That means even if you're not in the scene, you need to be engaged. I'm looking at you, fellas," Lance says with a point at Knucks, Rob and Brent, before hopping off the stage and walking over to greet his unwanted guests.

"I had no idea you were such a task-master," Dwyer says with a disconcerting air of pleasure.

"I try to be tough, but fair," Lance replies, suddenly feeling as though he just entered into another job interview.

"You've met my wife, Sheila."

Lance nods. "Pleasure to see you again; my apologies for that dinner interruption at the club. Hank is very forward."

"That's alright, it was a nice break from the silence," Sheila icily replies.

Lance offers up a nervous, fake laugh as Dwyer smiles with joyless, anxious eyes and says, "Sheila is known for her crisp sense of humor."

Sheila raises an un-amused eyebrow at Dwyer, then pulls a book of crossword puzzles and a pencil from her purse and exits the conversation. Lance watches with triumphant pleasure as he realizes the man who had seemed to be a fearsome monster, is really just a sad man in a loveless marriage.

"Is it okay if we watch the rehearsal? I'd love to see the run-through. Tree gave me the overall synopsis and it sounds like a wonderful play," Dwyer earnestly says.

Lance's fleeting pleasure at the former monster's marital plight quickly turns to guilt as Dwyer's genuine interest draws empathy from within Lance, who clears his throat and says, "Of course, be our guest."

Dwyer nods with gratitude and says wistfully, "You know, back in my San Francisco days, I actually took some theater classes at A.C.T. I always wondered what my life would have been like if I had pursued the arts. Maybe things would have been different…" Dwyer glances at Sheila, lost in her crossword puzzle. The sight of her snaps him out of his brief moment of reminiscing and he apologetically says, "Sorry, didn't mean to sound like some self-obsessed weakling. You have a rehearsal to lead. Go."

"Definitely. Hope you enjoy it," Lance says with a nod and walks back to the stage in a daze. He pulls himself up onto the stage, walks over to Tree and whispers inquisitively, "Did Dwyer have some sort of near-death experience I didn't know about?"

Tree chuckles. "Not that I know of. Why?"

"He just seemed… Like a human being."

"That's because he is a human being."

"Yeah, but you know what I mean. A human being who isn't constantly acting like a Bond-villain."

Tree laughs. "Yeah, I can't say he's a particularly beloved guy, but behind all the drill-sergeant crap, there's a good heart with a lot of achin' inside. Honestly, I feel for him. If you can believe it, he's the sweetheart in that marriage."

"Yikes."

Emmy swats away a cluster of gnats as she walks through the dark backyard and knocks on the wooden fence separating their yard from Art's. Just after the knock, Art stands up, looks over the fence at her like Wilson in *Home Improvement* and asks, "What's the word?"

"Well, the good news is, the tracker is working to perfection. The bad news is, unless he's been meeting them at Mustang Donuts, there's been no suspicious activity."

Art chuckles. "Yeah, he'd know better than to meet at Mustang's. That right there is what you would call an Altitude employee hot spot. But it's only been a couple days, I wouldn't expect any contact to be made that quick."

"Agreed. As long as he and they don't know we're following him, it'll just be a matter of time. And if you have anyone you know you can trust, I think you should go ahead and have them sit on Ronald during the day. I'll set my tracker to alert me if he goes anywhere at night, but just in case he uses alternate forms of transportation, we'll be covered."

"Boy, I sure am thankful God blessed you with that baby. If you were still chasin' down criminals in San Francisco, I'd be up shit creek without a paddle right now."

Emmy suppresses a flattered laugh and deflects. "Oh, stop, I'm barely doing anything. But I'm thankful too. We'll win this battle, I know it."

Back at the rehearsal, Jack, in character as Officer Palladino, hides behind a foam streetlight and watches with jealous envy as Officer

O'Hanlon (Lance) and Laura (Judith), hold hands and walk in the opposite direction, exiting stage left.

"Intermission!" Lance shouts on his way back to the middle of the stage. Everyone in the auditorium applauds, aside from Sheila, still engrossed in her crossword puzzle. "We're going to take a fifteen-minute intermission, no more, no less, just like we will on the big night," Lance announces.

Tree waves his hand and mouths, "Gun," to Lance.

Lance nods. "Of course, thank you, Tree; I need Jack, Ronald and Judith to join Tree and I in the prop room."

All named parties swiftly make their way to the prop room. Tree opens a cabinet, pulls out a locked metal box, places it on the table, pulls out a key and unlocks the box. "Feast your eyes on the 1950 Colt Commander," Tree says ceremoniously as he lifts the lid and reveals a classic black pistol with a textured brown grip panel. He pulls it out, hands to Jack and says, "Vincent Palladino's weapon of choice."

Jack holds the pistol for a moment and asks, "Is this thing real?"

Tree chuckles. "Absolutely not. It's a replica gun. Built to look and feel exactly like the real thing. They even weight it so it feels loaded, but it can't actually fire bullets. We'll have your cue line for the gunshot set with our sound guy so we don't have to worry about any liability."

"That's a relief," Jack says with a laugh, then hands the gun to Judith.

"And same thing on your end, Judith. When you steal the gun from Vincent after you realize he's killed Conor and you fire that warning-shot, it'll be the same thing with your cue-line," Lance says.

Ronald leans in and points a thumb at Judith, "You should see this one handle a gun. I had no idea I was married to Annie Oakley."

"Wow, a beauty queen and a marksman? Impressive," Jack says to Judith.

She smiles. "I'm full of surprises."

Judith hands the gun back to Tree, who places it back in the box and says, "Our prop guy will be on top of everything throughout the night, but just so you know, the gun will be placed on Jack's section of the prop table during intermission so it's ready for you to hide it in your jacket."

"Beautiful, thank you, Tree," Jack warmly replies.

"Very helpful," Judith says with a smile as she softly pats Tree on his muscled shoulder.

When they return to the stage, Lance looks at the time and shouts, "Ten-minute warning!"

Dwyer stands up from his seat, approaches the stage and quietly says to Lance, "Can I have a moment of your time?"

Despite the earlier humanization of Dwyer, Lance still feels a flutter of anxiety in his stomach as he walks over to the dour administrator, hops down to his level and asks, "What's up?"

"It's about the quality of your play..." Dwyer replies in a tone suggesting the vanishing of any hint of his previous softening.

Lance sighs. "I know, we still have a long way to go, but we'll get there."

Dwyer shakes his head, clenches his fist and says, "No. It's fantastic."

"Really? You mean that?" Lance replies, thoroughly puzzled.

"I always mean what I say. Sarcasm is for the weak," Dwyer declares in total seriousness.

"Well, I really appreciate that. Seriously."

"I just call balls and strikes. No matter what I think of you personally, if you have a good product, I'm going to tell you. Now, would it be possible for me to take home a copy of the script? I'd like to really dig into your writing style."

"Uh, yeah, I have a whole box of them. Just give me a sec," Lance says as he hops back on stage and heads for the box of scripts, still in a daze from the shock of Dwyer's praise.

While Dwyer waits, Ronald shuffles over to him and offers a jovial greeting. "The great Mr. Vernon! How many Saturdays do I owe you again?"

Dwyer clenches his teeth as he slowly turns his head to Ronald and replies, "I don't enjoy the sound of your voice. I don't enjoy your small talk. Please, do not talk to me."

Ronald laughs, pats Dwyer on the back and says, "Man, your Vernon impression is so good! Gets me every time! Have you thought about auditioning for *Saturday Night Live*?"

As Dwyer weighs the consequences of physically assaulting Ronald, Lance returns with the script, hands it to him and says, "Thank you again for the kind words."

"You're welcome," Dwyer replies, then glares at Ronald with disdain for a moment before returning to his seat.

Ronald chuckles at Dwyer and says to Lance, "That guy is hilarious."

Chapter Nineteen

Day 130 of Pregnancy, One Week Until Showtime

Lance and Emmy sit on the living room floor doing pre-natal yoga. Duke jogs downstairs in his workout clothes and smirks at the contorted duo below him.

"Addaboy, Lance. Keep her in shape."

Emmy lets out a deep, mindful exhale and says calmly, "Keep talking, Duke. You're just adding to the nine months-worth of ass-whoopings coming your way as soon as I give birth."

Duke laughs mockingly at Emmy as he looks at their current pose. "Is that even a workout? Looks like you guys are just sitting on the floor."

"Why don't you come give it a try, hot shot?" Emmy replies through another exhale.

"Fine," Duke walks into the living room, takes a look at their current pose and attempts to recreate it, but quickly realizes that his heavy, muscle-bound frame and un-flexible limbs are not conducive to the exercise.

Lance looks over in amusement at Duke's struggle and asks, "You want some pointers there, Bud?

"I'm good," Duke says with a grunt as Emmy laughs tauntingly.

After a pained couple of minutes, Duke gives up and sits on floor. Soon after, Lance says to Emmy, "Let's take a break to hydrate."

"But I was just getting started!" Emmy says as she comes out of the pose and sits up. "You don't think I'm a weakling like my brother, do you?"

Duke scoffs, "That's a garbage workout. It's just a matter of how light you are. Lance, why don't you come to my gym today and I'll show you a real workout. Free of charge."

Lance shakes his head. "Sorry, my dance card is full. I have a Rosary session with your mom when she gets home and after that, I'll be prepping for dress-rehearsals all day."

"Excuses, excuses."

"Speaking of excuses, are you coming to the play next Saturday?" Emmy interjects.

"Of course, I am. You think I'd miss a chance to stare at Judith for two hours?"

Emmy rolls her eyes and turns her attention to Lance. "How are things coming along? Is the cast still looking strong?"

"Still strong! Although, as expected, Willie Nelson has lost some of his passion after his lady-part was cut."

Duke scrunches his nose and says, "His lady-part?"

"Yeah, out of context that's an odd sentence. He was supposed to also play a woman, but we had to eliminate that role, which pissed him off, but overall he's still been solid as the postman."

"How's everyone else doing? How's Ronald? How's Jack? Give me the scoop!" Emmy excitedly asks.

"Well, Ronald is doing great. He may be annoying, but he's a genuinely skillful actor and he's perfect as the wacky bakeshop owner. Initially, I was skeptical about Jack playing Palladino, because what woman in their right mind would reject that face? But the further we get, the more I realize that it actually adds to why his character would be so maniacal about getting rejected. A brilliant detective with stunning good looks like that doesn't get rejected too often and you could see how that would drive an unstable man mad. As for the smaller roles, Tree is awesome as the police sergeant. Although, even if he was terrible, he built the most incredible set I've ever seen, so he'd get a pass. Andres is bringing a much sassier take to the coffee magnate role, but honestly, I think it's better than how I originally envisioned it; adds some unpredictability and humor. I still don't know why those meatheads Knucks and Brent joined the theater club in the first place, but they're basically just playing menacing goons, so it's not much of a stretch. The third meathead, Rob, seems to genuinely be interested in acting, but every time I feel like I'm breaking through with him, the other two come over and he suddenly turns back into a disinterested frat-boy, so who knows. But, all in all, it's a good cast!" Lance concludes his breakdown with a smile, intentionally omitting his thoughts on Judith in an attempt to avoid Duke's inevitable ogling.

"You forgot Judith," Emmy asks probingly.

"Did I? Whoops. She is a fantastic actor. I thought Ronald was being hyperbolic when he first pitched her, but she's the real deal."

"And she's super hot!" Duke adds.

Lance sighs. "Thank you, Duke."

"Do you think she's hot, Babe?" Emmy asks Lance with playful jealousy.

"Oh, boy," Lance whispers under his breath and says, "I think she is someone who people find attractive, but I'm not going to say she is hot."

Duke makes a whipping sound. "Just admit it, she's bangin', Bro! And get this, I've been training her and she is a dope boxer. I think she could even take you, Sis."

Emmy shakes her head. "Not a chance. I'd break her."

"She's tougher than you think," Duke persists.

Emmy stops to think for a moment, then muses aloud, "That's an interesting profile. A beauty queen with incredible acting chops who can box like a professional and for some reason decided to marry Ronald." She turns her attention to Lance and Duke and says, "Honestly, I always felt like I knew Judith, but with my two guys fawning over her, I may have to look into this woman of intrigue and find some flaws."

"For the record, I was not fawning. I was just stating an objective fact that other men find her attractive," Lance objects with righteous indignation.

"Well, do you objectively think she's more attractive than me?"

Before Lance can answer Duke interjects with a resounding, "Yes!"

Lance shakes his head. "Absolutely not. You are much more attractive."

Lance shuffles over to give Emmy a loving kiss, but before he can, she stands up and says, "I'm finding something on her."

"Come on! Why do you have to run background checks on every chick I'm into?" Duke asks pleadingly.

"She's married, Duke. You shouldn't be 'into' her."

Duke shrugs. "I'm only human, Esmerelda."

Emmy glares defiantly at Duke as she heads upstairs to her office.

"Will you at least tell me what you find?" Duke begs.

"Nope!" Emmy says before disappearing down the hallway.

After a moment of stunned silence, Duke turns to Lance and says, "I have no idea how you deal with her jealousy."

"She's not jealous, she's just… Inquisitive. And after how she was treated by her ex-boyfriend, I get it," Lance replies empathetically.

Duke makes another whipping sound. "Just admit it. She's crazy."

"She is not crazy and you should not be seducing married women."

"Wow, so you're on her side now? After everything we've been through?" Duke asks, genuinely hurt.

"We could've been through World War II together and I still wouldn't condone adultery."

"Thanks, Moses," Duke says with an annoyed roll of his eyes.

Lance chuckles, seeing an opportunity to further needle Duke. "It's not Moses' fault. He didn't make up 'thou shalt not commit adultery,' he just wrote what he heard from God."

"Wow, when did you become such an expert on *The Bible*?" Duke snidely replies.

Lance laughs out loud. "I'm pretty sure it takes a little more to become a biblical expert than knowing one of the Ten Commandments."

"Whatever. The bottom line is, I wouldn't even be the one committing adultery. That's on her."

"Okay, again, I'm no expert, but isn't there one about not coveting your neighbor's wife? In this case, she's literally your neighbor's wife…"

"Dude, honestly, you need to stop hanging out with my mom. I mean, you always were kind of a buzz-kill, but you're becoming obsessed with the same outdated morals that she constantly drones on about. I don't need all that in my life."

"Sorry, I forgot how progressive and advanced you are," Lance replies with bemused sarcasm.

"Apology accepted," Duke earnestly says, completely missing the sarcasm.

★★★

Lance breathes in the warm evening air as he walks down the driveway and over to his tiny car, parked on the opposite curb. Just as he is about to open the driver's side door, he is startled by the sight of a man frantically sprinting towards him in the distance and quickly realizes the man is Ronald.

By the time Ronald reaches Lance, he is dripping with sweat and breathing heavily.

"What the heck is going on?" Lance asks.

"This is bad. Really bad," Ronald replies, still out of breath.

"Just breathe, and then tell me what happened."

After a few moments, Ronald catches enough breath to say, "Willie Nelson just texted me that he's quitting the play. Apparently, he got offered a lucrative gig the same night as the play and he can't afford to turn it down. I offered to match whatever he was getting from the gig, but he said the gig is bigger than just the money."

Lance bites his lip in frustration. "Damn it. I had a feeling he was going to drop."

"What are we going to do? The play is in a week?"

"I should have booked us a couple understudies. This is on me."

"Hey, let's not play the blame game here, Sir Lancelot. This isn't *The Real Housewives.* We rise and fall together," Ronald replies, doing his best fearless leader impression.

"We just already have so much to get done in one week, it's a real setback to have to recast someone cold."

"I got it! Let's offer the role to Principal Dwyer! He does the most incredible impression of Principal Vernon from *The Breakfast Club*. That man is a true method actor."

"You know that's not an impression, right?" Lance asks, thoroughly puzzled. "That's actually who he his."

"No... Come on. That's got to be an act..." Ronald replies incredulously.

"It may be a façade that hides his inner unrest and sadness, but it's not an act and it's definitely not an impression of the principal in *The Breakfast Club.*"

A wave of genuine hurt washes over Ronald's body. He hesitates for a moment, then replies, "So, he was just being mean to me that whole time?"

"Yep."

"I don't think I can work with him," Ronald says with a sigh. He sits down on the curb, runs his hands through his hair and says without thinking, "I have enough sadistic jerks in my life as it is."

"You do?" Lance says curiously.

Ronald suddenly realizes that he can't explain what he just said without risking his life, so he forces a wacky smile, stands up and says, "Aaaand scene! Pretty good, right? I had you goin' there."

"You jerk, I was actually feeling bad for you."

"Goes with the territory when your best friend is a comedian."

"Of course. How silly of me. Now, can we talk about Dwyer? I don't want to have to direct that sadist either, but I think he's our best shot. I mean, he's been watching all of our rehearsals for the past week, he's been clearly studying his copy of the script and he's old enough that if we put a gray wig on him, he'll fit the crazy old postman look."

Ronald acquiesces. "I hate to say it, but you're right. Let's offer him the role. I just can't guarantee that I'll be able to provide my signature humor or positivity when he's around."

"Well, that would be a major loss. But it's a chance we have to take."

Ronald salutes Lance and begins to walk away, then stops, turns around and asks, "You think I could get a ride back to my place? I'm already moist and Judith hates it when I sweat through my clothes."

Jack wears a black overcoat and a grey fedora as he bursts into the stage apartment and rushes up to Lance, dressed in 1950s loungewear, and smiles at his partner.

Jack triumphantly declares, "*I've cracked the case, O'Hanlon!*"

"*I knew you would,*" Lance replies with pride.

"*It never made sense to me that Guzman was the guy. I know we found his fingerprints on the gun, but why would this rich coffee magnate murder his accountant in a bakeshop bathroom? He had to know there would be witnesses. Why would he take such a big risk? I can see if it were a crime of passion, but to just knock off an accountant? No way. And then of course the precision with which the killer shot poor Mrs. Blankenship after realizing she recognized him, suggests it had to be the work of a professional. But again, that shiny new Colt Commander that was used had Guzman's fingerprints on it and multiple witnesses confirming that he bought the gun a month prior to the shooting. So, how could this have happened?*"

"*How?*"

"*You still haven't figured it out? O'Hanlon, you might be the dimmest partner I've ever had.*"

"*Just tell me.*"

"It happened because the evidence was planted! The killer is a cop," Jack says, then pulls the Colt Commander replica from his trench coat and "shoots" Lance as a gunshot sound plays over the loudspeakers. Lance clutches his chest in panic and shock as he falls to the ground. Jack slowly walks over to Lance, stands above him and says, *"If I can't have Laura, no one can,"* then aims the pistol at Lance's head as a gunshot sound once again plays over the loudspeakers and the stage lights fade to black.

Judith grins in the darkness as she envisions her plan coming to fruition. After a few moments, the lights turn back on and the cast applauds the first successful execution of the shooting scene. Lance stands up and addresses the group, saying, "Thank you for your patience, everyone. I just wanted to get the sound and lighting cues set before we jump into a full run-through. Jack, that was perfect, top-to-bottom." Lance high-fives Jack, then gives a thumbs-up to the tech booth and says, "You guys nailed it too. Just like that, every time."

The back doors of the auditorium open to reveal Principal Dwyer, who walks through them and down the middle-aisle. For the first time, Lance is relieved to see his former tormentor. He looks over at Judith and says, "Let's take five before we attempt the final scene with you and Jack."

He jumps down from the stage and greets Dwyer in the aisle. "Can we chat for a sec?"

"I'm sorry I was late, but I figured if I waited until you guys were finished with the scene it'd be okay to come in."

Lance laughs. "Oh, yeah, that's no problem at all. I wanted to talk to you because I'm in a bit of a bind. Willie Nelson quit the play and since you mentioned you had some acting experience; I was wondering if you'd like to play the postman…" A glimmer of true joy lights up Dwyer's face, leaving Lance both touched and a little bit unnerved, as though he had just hand-fed a dangerous animal.

"I would be happy to play the postman. Thank you for thinking of me."

"My pleasure, thank you for jumping in last minute. We'll have to make some alterations to the costume, so for tonight, you'll be the only one not dressed the part, but we'll have it ready tomorrow night."

Before Dwyer can respond, he's interrupted by Ronald's boisterous laugh from across the auditorium. He closes his eyes and simultaneously moans and growls at the thought of working with Ronald. He opens his eyes and says to Lance, "I just have one request."

"I'll keep Ronald away from you."

"Thank you. If he calls me Mr. Vernon one more time, I walk and I will only speak to him when we are in a scene. Aside from that, I don't want him talking to me. I don't even want him looking at me."

Lance shoots an exasperated look at Ronald who inexplicably begins to sing, "Boogie Shoes," by KC and the Sunshine Band, to the rest of the cast.

Dwyer shakes his head. "I don't know if I can do this."

"Please, it's just a week. I get it, there are times I want to throw my shoe at him, but he's the reason this whole thing got started. It's just a week."

Dwyer chews on his cheek for a moment, then replies, "Fine. I'll suffer for my art."

Lance nods with gratitude as Ronald wiggles his legs in the background and sings, "*I wanna put on, my my my my my boogie shoes! Just to boogie with you!*"

Chapter Twenty

Day 131 of Pregnancy

Duke sneaks a lustful glance at a perspiring Judith as she steps off a treadmill and approaches the free weight area. "You ready for a round of twenty-one's?" Duke asks.

"Oh, I'm ready. Who do you think you're training?" Judith replies, then grabs a twenty-pound barbell and busts out a set of twenty-one curls, alternating between seven full curls and seven half curls.

"I know who I'm training, but I wish my sister didn't know more than me," Duke says with a roll of the eyes as Judith returns the barbell to the rack.

"What does that mean?"

"It's nothing. She just got jealous because Lance and I were talking about how beautiful and talented you are, so she ran one of her police-level background checks on you. Pretty stupid, right?"

Judith sneaks a silent, deep breath to calm her boiling rage and paranoia and playfully asks, "What'd she find?"

"She wouldn't tell me, which means she probably didn't find anything interesting. But I wouldn't take it personal. She does this with every chick I date."

"But we're not dating."

"I know, but I kinda told her I have a thing for you," Duke admits with a sheepish grin.

With the realization that her use of Duke is backfiring and with no further need of him, Judith suddenly grows ice-cold and says, "I told you, I am a happily married woman and you promised to be professional. I'm sorry, but this is our last training session."

"Judith, please! I'm a human being. I can't help feeling what I feel," Duke pleads as Judith turns her back to him and storms out of the gym.

Duke glances over at a smirking co-worker. "Keep laughin', Chuck! See what happens to your face."

★★★

Lance is in the midst of a pre-rehearsal acting workshop with Dwyer, who proves to be an eager pupil. Behind them, Tree continues to refine the bakeshop set. Just as Dwyer is about to run one of his scenes, Ronald bursts into the auditorium holding the Sunday edition of the Dallas Morning News and shouts with excitement, "We're famous!"

Lance braces for Dwyer's anger at his nemesis' interruption, but finds the principal to be looking at Ronald with a knowing smile.

Ronald pulls himself up onto the stage, briefly revealing the top of his unseemly butt-crack, and reads the lengthy article promoting Saturday's upcoming play. At the conclusion he adds, "And get this, I checked the ticketing app before I left, we sold three hundred tickets today!"

Tree pumps his fist and bawls out one of his signature, "Woo's!"

A look of shock runs over Lance's face. "Damn, I had no idea newspapers still had such pull in this town."

Tree raises an eyebrow at Lance and says, "You didn't hear? Tony Romo tweeted out the article to all of his followers."

"No, I had no idea… Why did he do that?"

Dwyer loudly clears his throat and slyly says, "I may have forwarded the article and asked him to spread the word. Initially, he was non-committal, but when he heard you guys are donating thirty percent of all ticket sales to the Children's Miracle Network, he was in."

"We're donating thirty percent?" Ronald asks with a nervous laugh.

"Yep," Dwyer replies, as if daring Ronald to say no.

"That's so great," Ronald replies with a forced smile.

Lance ponders for a moment; then says with an air of revelation, "So, you really are friends with Tony Romo…"

"Do you have dementia? That's why I didn't hire you."

"Yeah, but I thought…"

Dwyer squints at Lance like an interrogatory cop. "You thought what?"

"Nothing. Thank you so much for doing that. Really."

Ronald interjects, unable to contain himself, "I know I'm not supposed to talk to you, but that is so incredibly awesome that you are friends with Tony Romo! I love that man!"

"He is a great American," Dwyer replies with reverence.

"He sure is. Honestly, anyone who doesn't like Romo is a putz," Ronald declares, as Dwyer smiles in approval, his hatred of Ronald decreasing with every Romo complement.

Art wipes the corner of his mouth with a cloth napkin, carefully folds it and places it on the table before saying, "Lupita, if you ever decided to open a papusa restaurant, I would invest my entire fortune in it. Those are the best damn pockets of deliciousness I've ever had. I never get tired of 'em."

"You are too kind, Art. I'll put some in a container for you," Lupita says as she stands up and heads for the kitchen with satisfaction after another successful Sunday dinner.

Art turns to a sulking Duke and whispers, "So, what's her name?"

"What?" Duke responds, playing dumb.

"In my experience, a man only looks like you if he lost his fortune or lost his woman. You ain't got much of a fortune, so I'm assumin' it's a woman."

"It is. But I don't want to talk about it."

"Fair enough," Art says, then turns to the rest of the table, "I think I'll be turnin' in for the night."

Hank throws up his hands. "What? No poker?"

"Sorry, watchin' you take my money might give me indigestion and that meal was too good to risk the ol' bubble guts."

"Duke? Emmy?" Hank says to his kids. The former shakes his head and leaves the dining room without a word. The latter pats her father on the shoulder and replies, "Sorry, Dad. I'm not up for it tonight."

Hank sits back in his chair with a look of dissatisfaction as Lupita returns with a container of papusas and hands them to Art, who gives her a grateful kiss on the cheek, shoots a knowing glance at Emmy and heads on his way. Emmy stands up from the table, exits the living room and follows Art outside.

Art stops on the porch and turns to Emmy. "Hit me with it."

"What do you know about Judith?"

"Ronald's Judith? Hm, well, I know she and Ronald make an odd couple, but women do tend to have a variety of notions as to what makes a man attractive. I know she was a pretty successful model and a pretty unsuccessful cook when I last had dinner with them. That's about it, I guess. Where you goin' with this?"

"I ran a background check on her."

"Why'd you do a thing like that?"

"It's not important."

"She spendin' a little too much time with your man at them rehearsals?" Art says with a chuckle.

"I said it's not important," Emmy repeats with a cheeky glare, then gives her report. "First off, she's already been married twice and I don't think Ronald knows. Her first husband was a wealthy hedge fund manager who died in a helicopter crash. A year later, she married an oil tycoon who inexplicably did not make her sign a pre-nuptial agreement and after six months of marriage, she divorced him and he was forced to sell his company and liquidate his assets. Soon after that, he moved back to his hometown of Abu Dhabi and a year later he was killed in a mugging gone wrong."

"Well, I'll be damned. Good thing Ronald don't own any companies, but she does sound like a bit of a black widow…"

"And here's the twist: both the hedge fund and the oil company were sold to Lucid, a multi-national corporation that Judith had worked for prior to her two marriages."

A dark shadow washes over Art's face at the mention of Lucid. He takes a moment to catch his breath; then he quietly says with an unnerving note of formality, "Thank you for the information. I will look into Lucid and find out if they are involved in all of this."

"Is everything okay?"

"Yes. I just need you to not say a word to anyone about Lucid. I mean no one. Not even Lance. Whether or not they had a hand in Judith's marital fatality rate or in our affairs at Altitude, they're as dangerous as the drug cartels and as shadowy as the C.I.A."

"So, they're the group you've been warning me about all along?"

"One of them. There are a few. But for now, the less you know, the safer you are. I got everythin' under control."

Chapter Twenty-One

Day 132 of Pregnancy

J udith nervously clutches her purse as she walks down the dimly lit
hotel hallway, once again wearing her large sunglasses. This time,
however, the typically sensual swagger of her gait is noticeably absent as
she approaches Chet. He quickly sizes her up and asks, "You okay?"

"I'm fine. Just step aside."

"No can do. Give me the purse."

Judith sighs and hands him her purse. "Really? Like I'm stupid enough
to bring in a weapon?"

"Just doing my job," Chet flatly replies and rifles through her purse.

"This is ridiculous. I only brought it because I'm on my period. You
hear that? There is blood flowing from my lady-parts. Is that a thorough
enough explanation for you?"

"It's clean," Chet says as he hands her the purse.

"Yeah, I know it's clean. I just told you that."

Chet opens the door, ushers her into the pitch-black hotel room and
closes the door behind her.

She takes a deep breath and attempts to steady her nerves as the
spotlight is turned on.

"Why the long face?" The cowboy says with a smile in his voice.

"I think I blew my cover."

"Your cover? Or our cover?"

Judith's eyes, hidden behind the sunglasses, close in anxious agony as she replies, "For now, just me. But I think it's only a matter of time until Art puts the pieces together."

"How did this happen?"

"Well, Emmy's idiot brother, up until now, has been a wealth of information, but he fell in love with me and she got protective of him. Apparently, when she gets protective, she runs background checks like the little Narc that she is and we both know what's in my file. This is really bad."

The cowboy laughs out loud with an air of condescension. "Oh, Judith, this ain't nothin'."

"How is it nothing? The whole point was to keep us hidden from Art until after the sale."

"That was plan-A. But now that Ronald's on the board, there ain't much Art can do to stop us even if he tried. And either way, he was goin' to come ridin' in on his high horse at some point. The question now is, will he come in peace or will he be stupid enough to try and fight?"

"Does he know where to find you?"

"He does."

"Should we at least scrap the plans for the play?"

"No chance, Darlin'. Full-speed ahead."

"But if Emmy knows I'm connected to Lucid, whether or not Art figures it out, she'll make me the prime suspect as soon as we buy Altitude."

"So? Let her. You could kill Lance with your bare hands, in front of hundreds of people, and my lawyers would get you off easy as pie. Don't fret, Little Lady, just stick to the plan and you'll be flyin' a private jet to Beverly Hills in no time."

★★★

Lance and Emmy sit on the living room couch eating lunch and watching *Frasier* re-runs. Duke walks down the staircase holding his workout bag. Emmy looks over at him and says, "Mom wanted to know if there's room in your spin class today?"

Duke looks at Lance with confusion. "Do you hear something, Bro?"

"Very mature," Emmy replies as Lance keeps his eyes fixed on his lunch.

Duke continues to ignore Emmy as he heads for the door. "Alright then, Lance. Have a good day."

"You know, Duke, as much as I've been enjoying this break from having to converse with you, I am curious, why do I suddenly not exist?"

Duke turns and glares at Emmy. "Because you're a jealous, paranoid, bitch."

"What'd you just call me?" Emmy says as she stands up in defiance.

"That's not cool, Duke," Lance interjects, standing up and placing a calming arm around Emmy's shoulder.

"It's the truth. You're a bitch," Duke says combatively.

Emmy looks away for a moment, then attempts to bum-rush her brother, but is just barely intercepted by her husband, who warns, "Honey, you're pregnant! No fighting!" and manages to briefly calm his wife. He turns to Duke and says, "Really, Dude?"

"Really. Judith doesn't want to train with me anymore because of her little background check."

Emmy's anger quickly turns to pragmatic anxiety as the idea of Judith knowing seeps in. "You told her about that?"

"Of course, I did. When it comes to my women, I'm not about secrets."

"Oh, my Lord! Listen, you're either delusional by thinking that she's interested in you when she isn't; or if she actually is interested in you, then you're both despicable because she's a married woman and Ronald is our friend. Not to mention, if you saw what I saw in her records, you'd be thanking me."

Duke's curiosity is suddenly piqued. "What'd you see?"

"Yeah, what did you see?" Lance adds. Emmy shoots him a questioning glance and he clarifies, "I'd like to know if I'm directing a monster. That's the only reason I asked."

"Let's just say, her previous marriages ended very poorly for the men she was married to…"

"What happened?" Duke asks, hanging on every word.

"I've said all that I'm going to say. But if I did ruin your chances at some sort of romantic relationship with her, I did you a favor."

"We gotta warn Ronald," Duke says with concern.

"Weren't you just trying to break up his marriage?"

"Yeah, but I didn't want anything bad to happen to the guy."

"Listen, you cannot say a word to Ronald about the background check," Emmy warns.

"What's in it for me?"

"Well, it will prevent me from punching you in the balls while you sleep."

"Deal," Duke says, then opens the front door and bounds out of the house.

Lance turns to Emmy and asks, "Have you been holding out information from your deputy?"

"Yes. And I'm really sorry, but for now, I can't tell you any more details than I already have. Don't worry, I'm safe, but Art made me promise and this is one I have to keep."

Lance is about to protest, but something about the pained look in Emmy's eyes prevents him from inquiring further as Frasier Crane sings in the background, *"Hey Baby, I hear the blues-a-callin' tossed salad and scrambled eggs."*

Chapter Twenty-Two

Day 136 of Pregnancy

A rt drives his classic red Shelby Mustang North on the single-lane Highway 377. His heart begins to pound as he takes the left turn onto Surveyors Road in Krugerville, just minutes away from his destination. During the day, the thick clusters of trees on either side of the street would give him the feeling of relaxed joy that always came with drives through nature, but on this dark night, they only further contribute to the ominous feeling in the pit of his stomach.

After a few more turns, Art pulls up to the gate of a secluded, sprawling country mansion. He reaches out his hand to press the intercom "call" button, but before he can press it, the gate opens. Art takes a deep breath and drives through the gate, into the dark courtyard. He looks around and notices that although there are plenty of light fixtures lining the driveway, all of them are out and no lights are on in the mansion, leaving his headlights as the only source of illumination. As he approaches the house, he looks closer and sees that all the windows have been boarded up. For a moment, he questions whether the mansion is still owned by who he thinks it is, but that question is quickly put to rest when his headlights reveal a giant, stone sculpture of an owl in front of the house.

He slowly pulls up to the owl, puts the car in park and cuts the engine. After a few moments of silent prayer, Art looks up and catches a glimpse of his reflection in the rear-view mirror. "Damn, you've gotten old, Partner," he says to the grizzled face staring back at him, then grabs his Colt Python Revolver out of the glove box, loads it with ammunition and grunts as he climbs out of the car.

The sound of crickets and katydids fill the air as Art reaches behind his back and carefully places the revolver between his belt and the waistband of his faded dungarees. He takes a look around and surveys his surroundings with the practiced eye of a former marine. Satisfied that the coast is clear, he walks up to the front door of the mansion and is about to knock, but like the gate, it opens automatically. He hesitates for a moment then steps into the dark mansion and looks around at the odd, but familiar surroundings: a classically furnished, slightly run-down, empty hotel lobby.

Emmy looks out her living room window and sees Art's back patio light on. Hoping to catch him out there, she puts on her flip-flops, opens the sliding glass door and heads into the backyard. She loudly knocks on the fence as she squints through a tiny gap, hoping to catch a glimpse of him. After a few silent moments, she walks around to the front of the house and makes her way over to Art's house, finding all the lights off and the door locked. She rings the doorbell just in case, but gets no response and heads home.

Back inside, Emmy walks over to Hank and Lupita, cuddled up on the living room couch, watching *Bridge of Spies*. She grabs the remote, pauses the film and attempts to hide her concern as she asks her dad, "Have you seen Art?"

"He said he had a work thing," Hank says, then reclaims control of the remote and presses play.

Emmy breathes a sigh of relief as Lupita beckons. "Why don't you join us, Esmerelda?"

"I don't know, I have a lot of work to do."

"It's Tom Hanks," Lupita says with a tone suggesting that in their home, you don't snub Tom Hanks.

Emmy takes the hint, grabs a blanket and settles into her cushy armchair for a much-needed evening of relaxation.

Despite Tom Hanks' calming presence on screen, the film's foray into espionage reawakens her nagging suspicion that something is amiss with Art; that maybe the "work thing" Hank referred to could have something to do with Lucid Corp.

The walls of the fake hotel lobby are painted blood-red, with kitschy Texas-inspired memorabilia hung throughout. Art's cowboy boots slowly walk on the matching blood-red wall-to-wall carpeting, almost as though he is wandering through a human vein. Despite the urge to turn around and drive home, Art continues to methodically make his way towards the large, opulent, golden staircase, leaving no corner unchecked. He passes the entrance to a darkened ballroom and looks up at the sign overhead that reads: "WELCOME TO THE NETWORK! WHERE DREAMS BECOME REALITY!"

Art climbs the staircase. When he reaches the top, he turns to his right and walks down a long, dimly lit hallway, glancing at each door number as he passes, looking for room 234. Art stops for a moment to examine a dusty painting on the wall that reads: "DALLAS: BIG THINGS HAPPEN

HERE." After a few moments of dissatisfied staring, he shakes his head and says to himself, "This ain't Dallas, this is Hell."

Art continues his search, reaching the end of the hallway, turning left and walking down an even dimmer hallway, at the end of which stands a young, muscular man in an expensive suit. Despite the danger that the large guard poses, Art finds himself oddly comforted by the sight of another human being.

When he finally reaches the guard, Art offers a polite nod and says, "Howdy, name's Art. I'm here to see your boss."

"I know who you are. I know why you're here."

Art takes a moment to examine the face of the guard. "Wait, is that Lil' Chet?"

"No 'little,' just Chet," he responds, clearly not pleased at being recognized.

"Well, I'll be damned! Last time I saw you, you were playin' Little League. How'd your uncle rope you into this racket?"

"Enough chit-chat. Are you armed?"

"I think you know the answer to that."

"Then I can't let you in."

"You think I came here for a fight?"

"I don't care why you came. I'm taking your weapon."

The two men stare each other down in silence for a few tense moments before Art breaks it, saying, "Listen, I am either goin' to walk in there just as I came, or I am goin' to leave here just as I came. I ain't here for trouble, I just want to have a conversation, but I can't talk unless I have proper protection. You understand?"

Chet looks away for a moment as he thinks it over, then opens the hotel-room door and says, "In."

Art tips his cowboy hat to Chet as he walks into the pitch-black fake hotel room. Chet closes the door behind him as the spotlight is turned on an unsuspecting Art, who shields his eyes and shouts, "Gollee! The hell is wrong with you?"

The cowboy lets out a long, menacing laugh. "Welcome to paradise, Art."

Art regains his composure as he adjusts to the blinding light and replies, "We have very different definitions of paradise. Always have. Always will."

"Ah, yes, your false vision of a perfect world beyond space and time. Pissin' your life away while we do the hard work of perfectin' this world. The real world."

"Perfectin'? Ain't nothin' perfect about murder and corruption."

"It's all for the greater good. The larger plan. You need to crack a few eggs to make an omelet."

"I'd rather eat a crap sandwich than your omelet. And what's with the theatrics? You too scared to face me man-to-man?"

The cowboy cackles. "Still clingin' to that ol' antiquated machismo I see."

"Listen, I ain't here to banter with you, I'm here to tell you to back off. Stay away from my company and stay away from my family."

"And what exactly are you going to do if I refuse?"

"I'll go public. I'll call every news outlet in the country and tell them what goes on in the shadows of your little network."

"See, now that would be a very bad idea. Not only would I make sure you died before you could say a word, we would have no choice but to kill everyone you hold dear and manufacture some pretty horrible stories about you that no one could refute."

"You make one more threat to my family and I'll make sure it's your last."

"My apologies, no more threats. Although, do you consider Lance Ford your family? I mean, the husband of your goddaughter is pretty far removed..."

Art's blood runs cold at the mention of Lance and Emmy. "You stay away from both of them, ya hear?"

"Of course. *I'm* stayin' far away from them. Judith, on the other hand, has some plans for that San Francisco queer."

Art suddenly whips out his revolver, shoots out the spotlight and with the quickness of a man half his age, reaches behind him, turns on the hotel lights and crouches behind a nearby dresser. He glances in the direction of the now-shattered spotlight and realizes that what he thought was the cowboy, was actually a large, professional speaker with a video camera sitting atop it. He curses at himself for falling into the trap as he points his gun at the hotel-room door, expecting Chet to enter, guns blazing.

After an excruciatingly long minute passes, Art slowly makes his way to the door, opens it up and quickly steps to the side, with his back against the wall. After two quick glances into the hallway, he finds it empty and exits the room, gun at the ready. Thoughts of Lance and Emmy in danger flood his mind as he realizes the need to get back to Dallas as soon as humanly possible. He trots to the end of the hallway, pauses at the corner and quickly peaks his head around it. Suddenly, the chorus from "Happy," by Pharrell Williams begins to blare on repeat from invisible speakers throughout the hotel. Art grimaces at both the extreme volume of the song and the extreme annoyance of its content. After confirming the second hallway is clear, Art swings around the corner and attempts to resume his trot, but the moment he pulls even with the dusty painting of Dallas' slogan, Chet dives out from the false ceiling and lands on Art, knocking him to the floor and flinging the gun out of his hand. Despite Art's unusual strength and quickness for a man his age, the element of surprise and Chet's prodigious power combine to overwhelm his defenses as the two men grapple. After a short struggle, Chet manages to place Art in an expert chokehold designed to quickly render an opponent unconscious. Just before blacking-out, Art feels Chet's forearm shift to allow the long, calloused fingers of the cowboy to grip his neck and shove a needle into it, injecting him with a large dose of Propofol.

"Take him to the dungeon," the cowboy orders as Chet stands up, grabs Art and tosses his limp body over his shoulder.

"With his reputation, I was hoping he'd put up more of a fight," Chet says with a sinister chuckle as the two men walk down the hall toward the golden staircase.

Chapter Twenty-Three

Day 137 of Pregnancy

A slim, hooded figure dressed in all black with a mask to match, moves swiftly through the North Dallas High parking lot in the early morning darkness and makes its way to the nearby auditorium, easily disabling the alarm with its gloved fingers and slipping inside.

The figure glides along the wall of the auditorium, up the steps to the stage and straight through to the back, passing the dressing rooms and opening the door to the prop room. Once inside, it flicks on the light and removes its mask, revealing the face of Judith. She opens a cabinet, pulls out the prop-gun box, easily picks the lock and lifts the lid, revealing the replica Colt Commander. A pang of guilt suddenly hits Judith as she ponders the kindness with which Lance has directed her over the past month. For a moment, she considers leaving the fake gun in the box and running away to some far-off island where she can start a new life without any danger of being found by the network. This unexpected return of her conscience renders her temporarily breathless as images of her life prior to Lucid come flooding into her mind's eye. She can feel the days when greed and power didn't drive her every move and life was not just one big chess game.

"You've come too far to stop now," Judith whispers to herself, but somehow the voice does not sound like her own; almost as if some other force is driving her every word and action. "Keep your eyes on the prize. Think of Beverly Hills. Think of the studio job. It's the life you've always deserved," she whispers in that same hypnotic voice as visions of Rodeo Drive shopping sprees and star-studded parties successfully supplant the guilt-inducing images that her conscience had provided, snapping her out of the ponderous stupor and refocusing her mind on the task at hand. With measured efficiency, she removes the replica gun from its case and pulls a real, fully-loaded version of the same gun from her jacket. After hiding the replica in her jacket, she places the gun in the case, locks it up and returns it to the cabinet.

With the switch complete, Judith slips back out of the auditorium, re-arms the alarm and within thirty minutes is back in bed next to Ronald, still snoring in the same position he was when she left. Mission accomplished.

★★★

Emmy wakes up from a disturbing nightmare with a splitting headache. She looks to her left at an empty side of the bed, then stands up and quickly finds her headache also comes with a side dish: nausea. Although the second trimester has been easier than the first, she has yet to experience that boost of energy and vitality that her pregnancy books so often tout as a benefit of this middle phase.

After checking her phone and finding it devoid of any notifications, she gingerly walks out of the room and makes her way to the kitchen where she finds Lance eating breakfast and texting various people involved with the play. He stands up to give her a kiss and hug, then resumes his cellular correspondence.

As Emmy opens the refrigerator and attempts to find a breakfast that she can keep down, anxious thoughts of Art come flooding in again and she decides to postpone breakfast in search of her godfather.

After changing out of her sleepwear, Emmy heads over to Art's house and knocks on the front door. No Answer. She steps back from the porch and attempts to peek inside, but sees nothing and wishfully thinks aloud, "Maybe he had an early golf game… Dad probably hit the links two hours ago."

The cell phone in her sweatpants pocket begins to vibrate. She quickly pulls it out, but is disappointed to find the vibration is caused by her wake-up alarm, which she immediately silences, then puts in a call to Art, which goes straight to voicemail. She hangs up and tries again. Voicemail. This time she leaves a message, intentionally putting on a cheery tone in case the wrong people are listening. At the conclusion of her message, Emmy takes a step off the porch, thinks for moment before placing another call, this time to her dad.

Hank answers after one ring, "Hey, Honey. You better let Lance know, I'm beatin' the snot out of Dwyer this mornin' and I think he might be too ashamed to show his face in public tonight at that play. I've never seen him golf this bad. I think he has a case of the ol' butterflies."

The muffled sound of Dwyer's voice in the background interrupts Hank for a moment before Hank responds, "Oh, relax, since when did you care what Lance thought?"

Emmy interrupts the trash-talk and asks as innocuously as possible, "Is Art there with you guys?"

"Art? Uh, no, I asked him the other day if he was goin' to play this weekend and he declined. Why do you keep checkin' on him? There somethin' goin' on that I don't know about?"

Emmy sighs. "No, it's nothing, I just… Enjoy your game!" Emmy cheerily says, hanging up before Hank can question her further.

She takes a deep breath as she scrolls through her contacts and puts in a call to Jack. After a few rings, Jack answers the phone with a groggy, "Hello?"

The thought that her worries about Art could be unfounded once again pops into her head, bringing with it a sudden embarrassment at rousing Jack from his slumber, but she proceeds. "Sorry if I woke you up, I just wanted to see if you've heard from Art."

Jack coughs the sleep out of his throat. "His secretary left me a voicemail last night saying he was heading to Costa Rica."

"Costa Rica? What's he doing in Costa Rica?"

Jack laughs. "He's been trying to expand our flights there for the past year and I know he's getting close, so he must just want to relax for the weekend before digging into those meetings. Of course, Madison is pissed because she wanted to sit with him at the play. Actually, would you be cool to sit next to her and keep her company?"

Emmy breathes a sigh of relief. "I would love to sit with Maddie. And please let me know when you hear from Art. His cell phone has been going straight to voicemail."

"Yeah, he goes radio silent whenever he travels, but I'll keep you posted."

Emmy resists the temptation to question Jack about Lucid Corp. and instead concludes the call by saying, "Thanks. Break a leg tonight."

★★★

Vivid nightmares featuring a variety of persecutions torment Art during his twelve hours of drug-induced slumber. As his eyes slowly open, he is mercifully transported out of the current dream, one in which all four of his limbs were chained to the wall of a slave ship. Unfortunately, the more he takes stock of his surroundings, the more he thinks he may be in some sort of *Inception*-esque dream within a dream. Instead of the slave ship, he's now in a late nineteenth century Western jail cell, with steel bars in front of him and all four of his limbs chained to the brick wall behind him. This time, however, the pain and his surroundings feel much more real. Suddenly, a massive wave of nausea hits his body and sends vomit splashing onto the stone floor.

At the sound of the splatter, his jailer walks into the room; a man whose appearance further confirms Art's suspicion that he, in fact, is still dreaming.

The jailer looks with a clinical eye at the product of Art's nausea and says, "That's a side effect of the Propofol. Puking should take care of your stomach, but a splitting headache will be just around the corner."

A sudden migraine hits Art, confirming the jailer's assertion. Art winces as he looks again at the jailer and says, "You know, you look a hell of a lot like Willie Nelson."

The jailer chuckles and confidently replies, "I am Willie Nelson."

Art spits out some residual puke. "You ain't Willie Nelson. You're too damn tall."

"True, I'm not *that* Willie Nelson. But my name is Willie Nelson," he says earnestly. Suddenly an evil smirk comes over his face as he adds, "Although, if you look past the beard, the hair and the clothes, you might recall my former name."

Before Willie can finish his sentence, memories of the previous evening come flooding into Art's mind, further exacerbating his headache and leaving his entire body cold with dread, knowing that this is not a dream. His lip curls with pure contempt as he stares into the eyes of his psychopathic arch-nemesis and says, "Lars Cain. You miserable son of a bitch."

Lars cackles. "Yes, my momma was a bitch. I hated that woman. But, miserable? Not a chance. I'm ecstatic. This is damn near one of the best days of my life."

"Well, you look like a damn fool in that costume."

"Really? I think I look pretty good. Initially, I just did it as a lark. It allowed me to go undercover in my various companies like in that idiotic television show, except instead of giving sad sacks a pittance of cash at the end, I eliminated weak links. Boy, was it effective. So, I decided to make it permanent. Rule from the shadows and hide in plain sight."

"You always were a coward."

"So far, all you've done is insult the man who holds your fate in his hands."

"You don't hold my fate. The best you can do is threaten me with Heaven."

Lars cackles again. "That's comin', although I wouldn't be too sure about your destination. But before I kill you, I need to have a little fun." He pulls out an expensive cigar, lights it, takes a puff and blows the smoke in between the bars at Art. After a deep puff, Lars says, "Do you like my dungeon? I imported it from an old ghost town I bought in the nineties. I figured, if I'm goin' to imprison and torture folks, I might as well make it cinematic. We also made some upgrades."

Lars presses a button on the small table next to him and the slack on Art's chains begin to slowly tighten, pulling his arms up and out at an angle resembling a crucifixion. He looks back and attempts to resist, but they're connected to a powerful machine on the other side of the brick wall, leaving him helpless as his long arms are stretched painfully wide.

Lars watches the chains do their work with sadistic pleasure. "You looked a little tense, so I figured you could use a stretch. Now, I understand why you didn't tell anyone you were coming here. You knew that if you told anyone near and dear to you, they'd eventually come sniffin' around Lucid, which, of course, would be very bad for their health. The problem is, now no one knows where to find you. And you'd be amazed at what can be done with voice technology. Your dim-witted secretary had no idea that the man who called and informed her of your trip to Costa Rica, was not, in fact, you. And for good measure, your precious Mustang has been parked in your special spot at the airport by a man perfectly fitting your description, with all of your forms of I.D. and last night he took the red-eye to Juan Santamaría Airport and checked into a suite at the Marriott. So, as far as the world is concerned, you are safe and sound, enjoyin' the tropics."

Art stares in defiant rage as Lars continues, "Now, on to the larger task: Altitude. You really should have given up fighting after the leak. You had to know we were behind all the various sabotage attempts over the past few months and there's no way you were going to beat us. Stupid, stupid, man. You could have saved some lives."

"Who did you kill?"

"I didn't kill anyone. That's more Chet's department. He took care of Torlakson, but again, you had to know that. He never had the courage for suicide. You, of course, may have been spared if you went quietly, but then you rode in on your red Mustang like some Clint Eastwood wannabe. And tonight, Chet will be filming the play so you can watch Jack shoot your little buddy Lance and send your empire crumbling to the ground."

"Jack?" Art replies, fearing he had been betrayed.

"Before you get your panties in a bunch, he has no idea. My sweet little Judith will be swapping his prop gun for a real one. It'll be an honest mistake, but without your guiding hand, will the board really want someone stupid enough to fall for that running the company? I think not." Lars takes a few moments to enjoy his cigar before adding, "You know, I'm realizing, you actually did me a favor when you turned down my offer to join the network. Someone as naïve as you would surely sink us. I mean, you just appointed Ronald to the board! Which on its face is ridiculous, but considering he's the very man responsible for the leak, it's downright shameful."

With each bit of news, Art's angry, defiant demeanor slowly deflates; leaving him in pained silence as he contemplates his failure to prevent this catastrophe and the betrayal at the hands of Ronald, a man whom he viewed as a family member.

After another long puff of his cigar, Lars continues with a casual maliciousness, "You did get one thing right, it is indeed very dangerous to investigate us, and unfortunately, it has come to my attention that your goddaughter has been diggin' up dirt on Judith and, by extension, the network. I would bet that the dirt she found and passed on to you is what led you to the conclusion that I was behind the sabotage; which, of course, made you decide to come shoot out my spotlight. Again, the stupidity! So, she'll have to go."

Art bursts out in a fit of rage at the threat to Emmy's life. He pulls at the chains with all his might with a volume and force that would make you believe he could actually rip the wall down, but Lars quickly puts that thought to rest by pressing the button and further tightening the chains.

"Don't worry, I'm not killing her yet. That would be reckless. We'll let her have that baby first and then we'll go about turning that baby into an orphan," Lars says with a menacing laugh as he flicks his cigar in the screaming face of Art.

★★★

Hank turns around in his front-row seat and scans the packed auditorium. As his eyes reach Emmy, who sits four rows back with Madison, he gives her an excited thumbs-up and points at the sold-out crowd. In stark contrast to Hank's exuberance, Lupita sits next to him with her eyes closed and head bowed, deep in prayer. Next to her sits Duke, who glances at his mom and sighs with embarrassment at her public display of religiosity.

"Mom, can you please be normal tonight?" Duke whispers impatiently.

Lupita suddenly opens her eyes and turns to Duke. "You need to go check on Lance and make sure he's okay."

"What? No way! Lance is fine. He's a professional."

"I think he's in grave danger."

"Well, I'm not allowed to go back there and the play is about to start."

"Then I will go," Lupita replies curtly, but before she can stand up, the house lights go down and the curtains open. Duke holds out his hand to keep his mother in her seat as the audience gives a raucous ovation to the start of the play.

Ronald wears a classic baker's outfit as he slices a loaf of bread and looks up at the audience with a smile, saying, "*Well, hello there, folks. My name is Mr. Blankenship, I am the owner of this fine bakeshop, but you already knew that.*

Everyone in L.A. knows about my famous cookies and, sadly, our infamous double homicide." He wipes a tear from his cheek, places his knife next to the half-cut loaf of bread and continues, *"If only I had been there that day, maybe my dear wife would still be alive."*

Lance and Jack, dressed as detectives, await their cue to enter the bakeshop as Ronald milks his moment in the spotlight, weeping for an uncomfortably long, un-planned amount of time.

"I knew he was going to hijack the play," Lance mutters in frustration, already feeling control slipping out of his hands.

Jack looks over at Lance, sensing his anxiety, and places a strong, comforting hand on the anxious director's shoulder. "It's going to be great. Just have fun," Jack says, his simple confidence temporarily soothing Lance's internal strife.

Over the course of the play's first act, it is clear that Lance's moody crime drama is a hit with the excited crowd. Despite Ronald's transparent and repeated attempts to stand out with his over-the-top performance, Tree's portrayal of the police sergeant is clearly the fan favorite, both due to his strong acting and beloved status within the community.

After he finishes a tense, investigative scene with Jack and Andres, Lance peaks out at the crowd from the backstage left wing and watches Dr. Chung's husband in the front row, occasionally making notes for his column with a look of approval. Lance's feeling of pride at the reviewer's enjoyment is quickly balanced by the vision of an elderly man, seated just behind Dr. Chung, fast asleep with his head resting on his chest. He chuckles to himself and turns around to find Principal Dwyer rushing towards him.

"Lance, we need to talk," Dwyer says with conviction.

"You're supposed to be entering from the other side of the stage in like two minutes! What are you doing?" Lance replies, inwardly relishing at the license to tell Dwyer what to do.

"I know, but this is important. I just noticed some creep in the sixth row filming the show with a camera in his jacket. Did you authorize this?" Dwyer asks, unaware that Ronald has joined in on the conversation.

Lance looks confused and shakes his head as Ronald interjects, "This is awesome! We're already being pirated! I knew we were going to be famous."

Dwyer looks back at Ronald with contempt before walking with Lance to peak out into the audience at the man with the camera. Ronald follows them and sneaks his own peak, his blood suddenly running cold at the sight of Chet, seated in the sixth row, secretly filming the show.

"I have no idea who that guy is, but he shouldn't be filming," Lance says with frustration.

"I'll have a chat with him during intermission," Dwyer replies with relish at the opportunity to flex his authority.

Ronald nervously scratches his head and warns, "I would just let him do his thing."

"I will not tolerate unauthorized dissemination of our work. Now, if you'll excuse me, I have a scene to do," Dwyer emphatically replies before marching around the back of the stage to the other side just in time for his entrance, passing Judith, who glances at the prop guy as he carefully places the Colt Commander on Jack's section of the prop desk.

A few minutes later, the curtains close on the first act as the audience, many of whom are first-time theatergoers, cheer like football fans at their home stadium. Just before the house lights turn on, Chet stuffs the video camera securely into his jacket and stays seated while the rest of his row stands up to stretch their legs, buy refreshments and use the restroom. Suddenly, he feels a large hand rest on his shoulder and looks back to find the postman from the play staring down at him angrily.

"Did you get permission to tape this show?" Dwyer asks, hoping to intimidate the rogue videographer.

"First off, remove your hand from my shoulder. Second, I don't need permission. It's for my personal use," Chet defiantly replies.

"I don't care if it's for your cat, unless you have permission, you can't be filming us. I want to see you delete the files in front of me and surrender the camera until the end of the show or else I'll have no choice, but to escort you out," Dwyer warns.

Chet stiffens his upper lip as he slowly stands up and takes off his jacket, revealing the outline of his imposing physique and sending a rare pang of fear into Dwyer's heart. He stares menacingly into the postman's eyes for a moment, cracks his neck and says, "I'll do whatever the hell I want. You can try to escort me out, that's your choice, but it would be a bad one for your health."

"Fine, then I'll have no choice, but to call the police."

For a moment, Chet considers breaking Dwyer's nose, but the prospect of causing any commotion at this critical juncture causes him to nod with contempt and begin his exit from the theater. Dwyer follows close behind, feeling triumphant after his successful standoff, to ensure Chet fully leaves the building, but this only inflames the menacing man's anger. He turns back to Dwyer and asks, "What's your name?"

"Principal Dwyer. I run this place."

"Duly noted," Chet says with an unsettling smile as he walks out the side door and into the night.

Back in the lobby, Duke buys six cups of red wine, immediately gulping down three of them before carrying the other three back to his seat, handing one to each of his parents.

"Where is your sister?" Lupita asks.

"I saw her in the lobby eating cookies with Maddie. What's up?"

"Someone needs to check on Lance."

"Oh, come on, Ma, he's clearly fine! What could happen in a theater full of people?"

Lupita shoots him her signature glare as Hank leans over and says, "Duke, listen to your mother or else I'll start chargin' rent."

"Fine, I'll go check on Yoga-Boy," Duke petulantly replies.

"Thank you. And be nice to him," Lupita warns as Duke rolls his eyes, stands up and sneaks backstage.

Lance finishes his intermission address to the cast and walks in search of a brief moment of solitude, which he finds in a quiet corner backstage, next to the prop table. Just after closing his eyes, the sound of Duke's booming voice approaches him. "Yo, you good, Dude?"

He quietly moans with frustration at the interruption before opening his eyes and curtly replying, "Of course, I'm good. Why wouldn't I be good?"

"I have no idea. My mom kept pestering me to check on you. She's worried you might be in danger or something ridiculous like that," Duke says dismissively.

"Well, thank her for me and assure her that everything is okay on my end," Lance replies, hoping Duke will leave. Unfortunately, Duke doesn't take the hint and begins to explore the backstage area.

After sneaking a bite of one of the prop cupcakes, he scrunches his nose and says, "Ack! This thing is super stale."

"You can't eat those!" Lance says, rushing over and shooing his brother-in-law out of the main stage area and toward the backstage exit.

As they pass the prop table, the gleaming Colt Commander catches Duke's eye, stopping him in his tracks. Unable to resist, he picks up the pistol and examines it.

"Please don't mess with that," Lance begs impatiently.

"Is this real?"

"Of course not. It's just a replica. It's the gun Jack shoots me with."

"This ain't a replica, my brother. This is the real deal," Duke says with confidence as he releases the clip and shows it to Lance, "and it's loaded."

Lance stares at the gun, looking shaken. "Are you sure?"

"I'm sure. Someone's out to get you. Freakin' Mom was right, you're in danger!" Duke says, suddenly riled up with protective zeal.

Lance puts a calming hand on Duke's chest, "I appreciate your concern, but let's just stay cool and calm. We'll try and find out who did this after the play, but for now, I just want to figure out an alternative weapon and finish strong. We have a lot riding on this second act."

"Whoever did this better hope I don't get my hands on them. No one messes with my brother," Duke says, pacing around the small area like a caged tiger as Lance attempts to keep his composure amidst a flurry of emotions, the most surprising of which is the appreciation of Duke's brotherly love and concern.

The cast slowly begins to file into the backstage area, along with the stage manager and prop coordinator. Before Lance can address them, Duke steps forward holding the gun and exclaims, "Which one of you is the punk ass who planted this real gun to try and shoot my brother?"

"What happened to cool and calm?" Lance whispers to Duke as the shocked cast looks around with suspicion and Judith does everything she can to hide her disappointed rage and feigns a look of deep concern.

"I promise you; I locked a replica gun in that box," Tree solemnly replies with no trace of his typically jovial demeanor.

After the stage manager and prop coordinator make similar denials, Lance quiets the group and says, "Look, we're not going to find out who did this in the four minutes we have until the end of intermission, so let's just do this: Duke, if you don't mind staying backstage, I want you to hold onto the gun and the clip and when it's time for the shooting scene, just give Jack the empty gun. And Jack, if you can just cheat out a little bit when you shoot so the audience won't see that there's no clip. Deal?"

The cast nods as Duke rests his eyes on Knucks, Brent and Rob. Sensing a lack of concern for Lance, Duke calls them out, "Any of you three juiceheads know who did this?"

"Who are you callin' a juicehead?" Knucks says as he steps to Duke, nearly bumping chests.

Tree steps his giant frame in between the two men and pushes them both back as Lance emphatically says to Duke, "Listen, I need you back here, but I can't have you picking fights with my actors, got it?" Duke nods begrudgingly. Lance turns to the cast and says, "Everyone in the next scene, get to your places. For right now, I want you all to forget what just happened."

The cast immediately complies with his directive and a flurry of activity commences. On her way to the stage, Judith walks over to Duke and places a manipulative hand on his shoulder. "Thank you for finding that, Duke. I'm sorry I overreacted last Sunday. You're a good man."

In full war mode, Duke brushes her off. "Sorry, I can't flirt right now, Judith."

A few feet away, Ronald pulls Lance aside and says, "I think one of the rival theater clubs was behind this. They're jealous of our fame and want to sabotage our big night. I know it."

Andres overhears Ronald's suggestion and interjects with tears welling in his eyes as he places a hand on Jack's shoulder. "Don't be stupid, Ronald. If anything, I think it was about my Jack. So many people want to tear him down. They wanted to humiliate him."

"Andres, that's a little far-fetched," Jack deflects as Dwyer walks over and joins the conversation.

"I wonder if that creep with the video camera was involved. Now, I wish I hadn't thrown him out," Dwyer laments.

Lance quietly wanders away from the conversation, lost in thought with Lupita's warning echoing in his mind as it fully hits him that someone tried to get him killed. With the paranoia and fear quickly rising, Lance drops to his knees, places his forehead on the floor and reaches his arms to his feet in the relaxing rabbit pose. Suddenly, a surge of gratitude for Lupita wells up inside Lance as he attempts to remember the words to the various prayers she taught him.

Ronald looks over at Lance's yoga pose with an impressed smirk and whispers to Dwyer, "He's so Hollywood."

The drama of the intermission quickly fades into the background as the curtains open and the second and final act begins, leaving the scent of suspicion and fear floating around backstage. And despite the murderous origin of the cast's mood, it proves to be quite beneficial to their overall performance. As the events of the play unfold, the formerly raucous audience now stares in rapt attention, occasionally gasping at various twists and turns, most notably, Officer Palladino's murderous betrayal of Officer O'Hanlon, which leaves them floored. After Jack's perfect execution of the fake shooting, Lance lays flat on his back in mock-death, staring up at the rafters while the stage spins below him and stops, his set now facing backstage. Although it is safe to stand up, Lance takes a moment to process the surreal nature of the past hour and the possibility that this fake death could have led to his real death.

"Are you okay? He didn't actually kill you, right?" Duke whispers with concern as he helps Lance stand up.

Lance chuckles and whispers back, "I'm alive. Let's just enjoy the last couple scenes, shake a few hands and get home."

"Sounds good to me. And listen, until we find out who did this, I'm not leavin' your side. Just consider me your full-time bodyguard."

Lance offers Duke an appreciative laugh, truly touched by his concern, but wondering if being joined at the hip to him is a cure that's worse than the disease.

As the final scene of the play unfolds, the two men watch Judith point the gun at Jack and deliver her final monologue. Something about the look in her eye sends a chill down Lance's spine. Just as he's about to whisper to Duke his suspicions about Judith's potential role in the nefarious plot, Duke leans in and whispers, "I think she did it, Bro."

Lance whispers back, "Wow, I was thinking the exact same thing. I just have no idea how we prove it, but I'm sure Emmy will have some ideas."

"Bro, she's going to flip her lid. You think I overreacted? Just wait."

"You think we should call the police?"

"I wouldn't. They won't catch 'em and you'll just be stuck here for an extra few hours. Let my sister do her thing. She may piss me off, but if there's anyone who can crack a code, it's her," Duke says with a knowing chuckle as they watch Tree enter the stage from the opposite wing and arrest Jack, which draws a loud cheer from Tree's fans. At the end of the scene, the stage spins to reveal Ronald, standing behind the bakeshop counter in character.

He takes a bite out of a cookie before stepping out from behind the counter and addressing the audience. *"Well, there you have it, Folks. The dastardly Officer Palladino was arrested and our dear Laura is safe and sound. In the months that followed, Palladino was sentenced to life behind bars, but they never were able to find his accomplice and that steely Italian officer refused to divulge his identity. Where could this mysterious accomplice be hiding? Well, since we're friends, I'll let you in on a little secret. He's standing inside this very bakeshop, eating a cookie and speaking to you. Maybe someday they'll find him, but I sure hope not. For now, I'm going to close up shop, take a nice evening stroll and lose myself in the Purple Sky. Until the next murder, stay safe, people of Los Angeles."*

Ronald tips his fedora with an evil smile as the stage lights go down and the curtains close, ending the play. After a moment of silence, the audience roars with applause as the curtains open and the cast walks out one-by-one, drawing a standing ovation by the time they are all present on stage, taking their final bow.

Chapter Twenty-Four

Day 138 of Pregnancy

As the clock strikes midnight, Lance, Duke and Emmy pile into the tiny Chevy Spark and begin their drive home. Along the way, Lance and Duke brief Emmy on the events of the evening and she predictably goes ballistic, but quickly regains her composure and spends the rest of the car ride quietly putting the pieces together in her mind. When they arrive home, Emmy begins to divulge her theory and gives Duke a list of items to grab from the house. He nods dutifully and asks, "What do I tell Mom and Dad?"

Emmy sighs. "Just say that we're going to a surprise cast party at Ronald's house. Technically, that is where we're going, and it will be a party of sorts, so you won't be lying."

"Are you sure this is a good idea, Babe? Shouldn't we just call the police?" Lance asks with trepidation.

"If I'm right, and we do that, Judith may go to jail, but Art will be dead," Emmy soberly replies.

"What a night," Lance mutters under his breath as they continue to wait for Duke's return.

A surprising wave of nostalgia for their previous life in San Francisco hits Emmy. She looks guiltily over at her husband, strokes his cheek and says, "I'm so sorry. We never should have moved back here. I thought it would give us a nice, quiet life to raise our baby, but man was I wrong. When I was on the force, I got so conditioned to always being confident and firm in my convictions that I let it bleed over into our relationship. I railroaded you into this move and I'm sorry."

Lance softly smiles at his remorseful wife and shakes his head. "As much as I'd love to say 'I told you so,' I'm glad we moved. Granted, I could have done without the attempted murder and I do miss San Francisco every day, but honestly, I needed this journey. My selfish bubble, living off of you, was going to burst one way or another and I'm glad it happened before our son came along. I truly believe we made the right decision and I appreciate you giving me that push."

Emmy kisses Lance and whispers, "Thank you."

"Although, if we end up getting kidnapped or killed by some crazy secret society, I may change my tune a little…"

"Totally fair," Emmy replies with a chuckle.

★★★

Ronald excitedly pulls ingredients from the pantry and begins to prepare a celebratory dinner for Judith, who calmly sits on a stool at the kitchen island, sipping a vodka tonic and plotting her next move.

"Do you think we should go to Broadway or just sign a movie deal right away? Either way, I think once this review comes out, we're going to be on the fast track to stardom," Ronald says as he slices a tomato.

"Definitely the movie deal," Judith replies with full knowledge that he is delusional.

"I just wish I knew who tried to kill Lance. We'll definitely have to clear that up before we talk to any studios. You think it was Knucks? Doesn't really seem like his style, but with the leak not working—"

Judith interrupts, "Let's just enjoy the evening and think about all that stuff another time, shall we?"

"Of course. I'm so sorry. And you, my love, were absolute perfection up there. 'She had the beauty of Marilyn Monroe and the skill of Meryl Streep.' That's what they're going to write about you. Mark my words."

Suddenly, the doorbell rings, startling the couple. Ronald looks at Judith with concern as he walks to the front door and looks through the peephole, then turns and shouts back to Judith, "It's okay, it's just Emmy and Lance."

Before Judith can tell him not to answer, he opens the door and smiles at his two friends. "You guys here for a little after-party? I'm makin' my special pasta sauce."

"Sounds great," Emmy enthusiastically replies as they enter the house and follow Ronald to the kitchen. After greeting Judith, Emmy's demeanor shifts. Now, the friendly pregnant neighbor is in full detective mode, with Lance standing behind her attempting to match her level of intimidation, but lacking his stage costume, he doesn't quite stir the same level of fear.

"Whoa, the play's over guys. No more film noir needed here," Ronald nervously says to his guests.

Emmy stares at Judith for a moment and asks, "What do you know about Lucid Corp?"

Judith plays dumb. "Very little. I worked a few events for them back in my modeling days. Why do you ask?"

"Who wants a spicy meat-a-ball?" Ronald interjects with nervous sweat accumulating throughout his body.

Emmy ignores Ronald and continues to press Judith. "I ask because soon after Duke divulged my discovery of your ties to Lucid, Art mysteriously disappeared."

"Art disappeared?" Judith asks, genuinely unaware of this development.

"I heard he was in Costa Rica. I called his secretary on Friday to make sure he was coming to the play and she said he took a last-minute flight there," Ronald adds.

"I don't buy it. Maddie and I played soccer together for ten years. Never once did Art miss an important game. He knew how much this play meant to you guys and I don't believe for a second that he would miss it for some business deal in Costa Rica."

Ronald replies skeptically, "I don't know, have you been to Costa Rica? It's pretty nice."

"It is nice, but he didn't go. I also did some more digging and found out that the late Karl Torlakson was deeply in debt to one of Lucid's subsidiaries. And judging by Art's reaction when I told him you were on their payroll; I'd say that Lucid has been the saboteur all along. Then, during a play in which Judith and three other men with confirmed ties to Lucid are acting in, there is an attempt to shoot my husband; the real aim of which, I believe, was to humiliate Jack and cause chaos at Altitude, furthering Lucid's chances of acquiring the company after that failed leak. The only thing I can't quite piece together is why this enormous, multinational corporation, would be fighting so hard to buy an airline? Yes, Altitude is one of the most profitable and with their level of employee compensation, Lucid could make some major cuts and dramatically increase profits, but they could do that with most companies. So, why Altitude?"

Judith interrupts with the steady, sympathetic tone of a therapist, "Honestly, we are just as distraught as you are about what happened tonight. We love Lance, and it's unfathomable that someone would try to do that, but I think you're letting your emotions get the best of you with this whole Lucid conspiracy theory. We had nothing to do with that gun being planted and we have absolutely no idea where Art is."

Emmy turns to Lance and says, "She thinks I'm stupid."

"I don't think you're stupid, I just think you're being a bit irrational, that's all."

"Tell me where Art is. Now."

Ronald slams his hand on the cutting board and attempts to play the heroic husband. "Listen, I've heard about enough of this. We just put on one of the greatest performances in the history of theater and you're over here making baseless accusations. My wife would never do any of the things you're implying. Period."

Emmy smirks as she pulls out her figurative ace in the hole. "You sure about that? How much do you really know about your wife? Did she tell you about her two previous husbands who both mysteriously died after making deals with Lucid?"

Ronald turns his shocked gaze upon Judith and asks, "Is this true?"

Judith sighs with mock guilt. "Yes. I'm so sorry I didn't tell you. I just wanted you to love me." As usual, Ronald is putty in her hands and walks over to give her a hug. During their embrace, Judith uses Ronald's body to block their visitors' view as she stealthily opens a nearby drawer, pulls out a silencer-equipped pistol and steps away from her husband, pointing the gun at Emmy, saying, "Slowly remove that gun you have hidden, place it on the floor and kick it over here. Now."

Emmy bites her lip in frustration as she acquiesces to Judith's demand.

Judith sighs. "You have no idea how many times I protected you guys. Emmy, they would have killed you for investigating them if I hadn't covered for you. And Lance, they wanted to brutally murder you, but I convinced them to have Jack shoot you during the play, which left you with a damn good chance of survival."

Ronald stares at Judith with a bruised heart and a shocked head. "You really planted the gun?"

"Shut up, idiot," Judith snaps back, freed from her dutiful, loving wife act. She turns back to Emmy. "Now, because you couldn't just leave it alone, Art's going to die, you're going to die and Lance is going to die. But it won't be here. Ronald, grab the rope from the garage."

"No, I won't do it," Ronald says in weak-kneed defiance.

Judith rolls her eyes, picks up Emmy's gun with her free hand and points it at her husband. "Go get that rope and bring it back here. Now."

Ronald sighs and obediently walks to the garage.

"Judith, I know you have people that you're answering to. If you help us take them down, I'm sure you can get a good plea deal," Emmy says with a level of calm that Judith finds suspicious.

"You have no idea who you're up against. If I turn on them, I'm dead, plea deal or not," Judith replies as Ronald returns with a coil of thick rope as Emmy makes a secret signal with her nose.

Immediately after the signal, Duke, clad in his old college football pads, helmet and uniform, crashes through the window directly behind Judith and tackles her to the ground.

Ronald stares in shock as Judith screams like a woman possessed and musters a frightening level of adrenaline-fueled strength as she attempts to fight off Duke, who warns, "Quit fightin'. You got a better shot of breakin' outta Guantanamo."

Lance holds back Ronald as Emmy rushes over and carefully picks up both guns, pressing the silencer to Judith's head and saying, "Stop."

Judith goes begrudgingly still as Emmy pulls out a pair of handcuffs and fastens them around her wrists. After securing the cuffs, Emmy grabs the coil of rope and methodically ties up Judith's legs and torso.

Ronald fearfully watches Emmy and says, "I promise, I had no idea about any of that. Well, I knew about the leak, I was kinda forced into it, but never in a million years would I have been okay with hurting any of you guys."

"Tell me where Art is being held," Emmy commands Judith, ignoring Ronald's excuses.

"I told you. I have no idea," Judith replies in defiance as Duke pulls her up to her feet.

"Okay, who put you up to this?"

"I don't know."

"You're really going to make this hard?"

Ronald interjects, "She's telling the truth. We have no idea who he is, but I do know where to find him."

"Shut your damn mouth, Ronald! You're going to get us killed," Judith warns.

"Well, judging by your marital history, that was probably going to happen to me sooner than later, so I got nothin' to lose," Ronald says with a shrug.

"Should we call the police before we go?" Lance asks.

"Good idea, Deputy. We may need backup," Emmy says.

"I wouldn't do that if I were you," Ronald warns, "you're heading outside the Dallas city limits to Krugerville and odds are in that town you'll get a cop or two on his payroll. They'll give him the high-sign and he'll be long gone by the time you arrive."

Emmy stares for a moment at Ronald without detecting any deception and says, "Okay, take us there."

"Tight! Let's go crack some freakin' heads, Bro!" Duke shouts.

Lance looks at Emmy in fear and says, "Babe, this is too dangerous. You promised you'd be safe. I know you care about Art, but we don't need any more guns pointed at us tonight. Let's just call the cops and let them take care of it."

Emmy shakes her head. "No, we have to go. And we're not calling the cops. Not yet. Not until we've arrived. Duke, take her upstairs to the master bedroom, put her in the walk-in closet and barricade the door."

"I'm being held against my will! This is illegal!" Judith shouts.

"Can we get in trouble for this, Babe?" Lance asks with a look of worry.

"She won't want to have to explain how she ended up in that predicament, especially considering Duke was taking pictures of her before he burst through the window. Granted, it may be a tad extended, but in the end, it's still a citizen's arrest and we'll make sure she gets out of there and to the proper authorities."

Duke picks her up and carries her upstairs to the master bedroom, gently placing her on the plush, carpeted floor. As he grabs a chair and places it in the closet, Judith makes a last-ditch effort at an escape, seductively saying, "You know, if you untie me, we could have some fun. You could even keep the cuffs on me. I like a little danger in my love-making."

Duke picks her up and sits her upright in the chair, then squats down and leans his face into hers as though he is about to kiss her, but stops an inch away and whispers, "You know, before I became a personal trainer, I always wanted to be a cop. Unfortunately, I got bounced out of the police academy. They said I was too reckless; that I'd be a danger to myself and a danger to those around me. But you know what my biggest problem was? Beautiful women could manipulate me with ease. I'd see a pretty face and suddenly the law went out the door. For the past decade, I've resented their decision. But thanks to you, I now realize they were right. I'm at peace about it and I wouldn't untie you for all the sex in the world."

Duke stands up, walks out of the closet, closes the door and begins to work on his barricade as Judith curses at him from inside.

Emmy steers the Emmy-mobile with Lance in the passenger's seat and Duke anxiously leaning forward from the backseat as they follow Ronald's truck out of the neighborhood.

An hour later, they stop behind Ronald as he pulls up to the gate of a sprawling country estate, surrounded by high cement walls. Emmy looks back and addresses Duke like a commanding officer. "Stay on the phone with me the entire time you're out there and no hero stuff. I just want to get an idea of the property's layout and block the exit so there won't be any escape when the police arrive."

Lance looks down at his phone and frowns. "There's no reception out here."

An impatient Duke leans forward to catch a better glimpse of Ronald, who is overcome with fear and intentionally fumbling with the gate code. "What is taking him so long?"

"Focus, Duke. If you have no reception, I need you to be extra careful. Do not take any chances. These are dangerous people and we don't want to lose both you and Art. I hate that I can't go in with you, but the baby needs to come first."

"Yeah, Sis, you better keep your butt planted right here. And Lance, I know I promised to stay by your side no matter what, but if something happens to me, I want you to use my life savings to hire a bodyguard."

Emmy chuckles. "His life savings should afford you about a day and a half of security."

"Really? I'm tryin' to save my brother's life and you're takin' shots?"

Lance reaches back and appreciatively pats Duke on the shoulder. "Thank you. That means a lot, but you just stay safe so we don't have to worry about any of that."

Duke's patience hits zero. "This is taking too long. I'm goin' in."

"Duke, wait!" Emmy pleads as he grabs her gun, exits the backseat and climbs over the ten-foot fence with remarkable ease.

"I'll go check on Ronald," Lance says as he steps out of the Emmy-mobile and cautiously makes his way over to Ronald, who sits in the driver's seat, weeping uncontrollably.

Lance applauds. "Fabulous work, Kozlowski! Your method acting knows no bounds. Truly authentic, believable crying."

"I'm not acting," Ronald replies, telling the truth.

"Spoken like a true thespian. Daniel Day-Lewis would be proud. Now, listen, as much as I would love to continue to take in this brilliant performance, we really need your help getting in there. You don't even have to go in. Just open the gate. That's all. Then you can drive away and call the police when you get reception. Sound good?"

Ronald regains his composure and begins to play along with Lance's assertion that it was all an act. "How did you know that the crying was fake?"

"Oh, come on, a tough guy like you would never weep like that. Now, let's punch in that code."

"Thanks for being my best friend," Ronald replies with a forlorn smile as he types in the gate code.

Lance gives Ronald a brotherly pat on the shoulder before bounding back into the Emmy-mobile.

Ronald watches with terror as the Emmy-mobile speeds around him into the nightmarish compound. He once again begins to weep as he pulls out into the street and drives off into the night with no intention of calling the police.

Inside the gate, Emmy and Lance drive up the dark, winding path to the house and park in front of the giant owl. Lance is suddenly overcome with concern and fear for Duke. The same Duke who, up until a few hours ago, had been a source of torment for him, now causes an overflow of protective zeal within Lance. He turns to Emmy. "I think Duke needs my help."

"No way. If I'm not allowed to go out there, you're definitely not allowed to go out there."

"I'll be careful. I promise."

"This isn't a play, Babe. This is real. These people are killers."

"Look, Duke and your mom are the reason I'm still alive. I can't just leave him on his own," Lance says as he opens the door, evading Emmy's attempt to grab him, and hops onto the pavement.

Chapter Twenty-Five

Day 138 of Pregnancy (Continued)

B ack at the dungeon, Art slowly drifts in and out of consciousness; the thirty-plus hours without food and water and the constant physical and emotional pain are swiftly draining his life force as Lars sips a glass of whiskey and watches his inmate with a sadistic smile.

The silence is broken by the entrance of Chet, who takes a whiff of the malodorous cell and says with disgust, "The hell is that smell?"

"He couldn't keep his Propofol down. Puked as soon as he woke up."

"Why are you hanging out in here? It reeks."

"Every whiff just reminds me of the pain he's in."

"Well, I hate to break up the party, but we have a bit of a situation," Chet warns.

"A situation?" Lars asks without a hint of concern.

"Yeah, Ronald's door code was punched in and now there's a black S.U.V. in the driveway. Knucks and his crew should be here soon. Should I call for any more backup?"

"Oh, no, that would ruin all the fun. Have Knucks deal with the S.U.V. The other idiots can watch the prisoner and clean up the puke while we lay some traps."

★★★

The mansion's boarded windows and locked metal doors equipped with finger print technology prove impenetrable for Duke, who continues to search the dark exterior for a way inside. Duke peeks around the corner of the house and sees a light on in a bungalow behind the Olympic-sized swimming pool.

Duke swiftly makes his way over to the bungalow and peeks through a window. Finding no one inside, he creeps around, opens the unlocked door and enters. The swanky pool house he expected to find himself in is instead revealed to be an impressive security room, filled with a vast array of weapons and monitors. For a moment, he considers taking one of the rifles with him, but decides against it, feeling content with Emmy's pistol. After studying the floor plan of the estate, printed and posted on the wall, he turns to the security monitors and clenches his jaw at the sight of Art alone in a cell on one of the screens.

"I'm comin' for ya, Art," Duke declares before taking one last look at the floor plan and rushing out of the pool house.

★★★

Emmy winces as a sharp pregnancy pain sears through her abdomen. As the pain subsides, Ronald's face pops into her head and it dawns on her that with every passing moment, the likelihood that he called the police decreases exponentially. She checks her phone; still no signal.

Suddenly, a lone pair of headlights enter through the gate and head up the driveway. Emmy watches the lights in her rear-view mirror and quickly realizes they are not the lights of a cop car, so she rushes back to hide in the connected trunk, shielded by her jet-black tinted windows as the car parks nearby.

Emmy sneaks a glance and sees Knucks, Rob and Brent emerge from the car and stare at the Emmy-mobile with suspicion. A few tense moments pass before Rob and Brent head towards the house, looking thoroughly unenthused with their cleaning assignment as Knucks pops the trunk and pulls out a spring-loaded window breaker.

After further examination of the Emmy-mobile, Knucks stops at the passenger side backseat window and shatters it. Just as Emmy is about to pop up and aim Judith's silencer pistol at Knucks, the sharp pain once again hits her abdomen and forces her to retreat back to her hiding place while Knucks reaches in, unlocks the door and looks inside.

"Don't make me drag you out of there," Knucks warns, hoping to scare his prey out as he pulls a switchblade from his pocket, enters the backseat and begins to search the interior. Just as Knucks turns to the trunk, Emmy bites her lip to dull the excruciating pain and pops up from her hiding place, gun pointed in his startled face.

"Get out of the car, throw away the knife and lie down flat on your stomach," Emmy commands.

Knucks takes a moment to measure if he can throw the knife at her without getting shot, but her fundamentally sound positioning of the gun suggests that it is too risky.

"Now!" She shouts as he nods begrudgingly and complies with her orders.

Emmy keeps her gun pointed at him as she climbs over the backseat and steps out of the vehicle, placing her knee into the middle of his back and zip-tying his wrists and ankles, rendering him immobile.

Lance crouches down as he cautiously sneaks along the side of the mansion in search of Duke. As he turns another corner, he notices a loose board on a nearby, first-floor window and mistakenly assumes that to be Duke's point of entry.

After doing one last check of his surroundings, Lance wedges his body underneath the loose board, pulls open the unlocked window and slides down face-first into a dark room, landing with a thud on the smooth, cold marble floor.

As his eyes adjust to the blinding darkness, he lies still in momentary silence, listening for any movement in the room. Satisfied the coast is clear, he pulls his phone from his pocket, flicks on the flashlight function and attempts to get a feel for his surroundings. From what he can glean, he seems to be in a very large room with high ceilings and ornate, textured walls. Almost as though he fell into a Versailles dance hall. He continues to cautiously follow along the wall, reaching a corner and continuing to his right until his light shines on the familiar sight of velvet curtains above a stage floor. After some examination, he finds the stage to be taller and larger than the one his play was just performed on, filling him with an unexpected, irrational sense of envy that is so common in the world of performance art.

As Lance quells his envy and re-focuses on the task at hand, he turns and freezes in terror at the sight in front of him.

★★★

Rob angrily rolls a mop bucket into the jail cell and stops next to Brent, who holds a paper towel roll and stares with contempt at an unconscious Art. "This is the guy everyone was so afraid of? We had to do Ronald's dumb ass play because of some old cowboy?"

Rob soaks the mop and replies, "Bro, we're cleaning up puke and you're complaining about the play? Honestly, that was the first assignment I've actually enjoyed. I'm thinkin' if we don't get a promotion soon, I might try my hand in Hollywood. Just tell the whole network to peace out."

Brent shoots an incredulous look at Rob and dismissively says, "No, you're not. First off, you can't act. Second, if you're out, you're dead. Those are the rules."

Rob shakes his head with the look of a petulant teenager. "I'd rather die than smell this nasty ass jail cell one more second. I'll be in the car." Rob throws the mop down on the concrete floor and storms out of the cell.

"Really, Dude? Now I gotta clean this up all on my own?!" Brent shouts after him.

"I'll send Knucks down to help you," Rob shouts back from the stairwell.

Brent glances over at Art with disdain. "Stupid old man," he says before grabbing the mop in frustration and hitting Art in the stomach with the wet, business end.

Art's eyes slowly open and consciousness painfully returns as the smell of bleach fills his nostrils. He looks over at the large, blurry man in his presence and attempts to clear his vision as the sound of footsteps again echo through the stairwell.

Brent keeps his eyes on the task at hand, assuming that Rob has regained his composure and the footsteps are his. "I'm glad you came to your senses, my man. Let's just finish this shit and get out of here," Brent says, looking back up at Art with disgust.

Just as Brent is about to pop him again with the mop, Art's squints as a second large, blurry figure storms into the cell.

Brent swings his head around just as Duke's powerful fist collides with his jaw, followed by two more haymakers and a swift knee to the stomach, knocking the wind out of Brent and dropping him to the floor, where Duke immediately lands on him and zip-ties his limbs.

"Please tell me this ain't a dream," Art whispers to Duke.

"It sure ain't," Duke says with a smile as he begins to search the room for a key.

"That control panel on the table is how you work it, I think," Art says.

Duke presses one of the buttons and immediately Art screams in pain at the tightening of the chains.

"Sorry! Wrong one!" Duke says as he urgently presses the opposite button, loosening the chains. He then presses four more buttons, each unlocking one of Art's limbs, leaving the old man slumped on the ground as blood rushes back to his arms.

"Let's get the hell out of here," Duke says as he rushes over to Art and helps him up.

"Just be careful, the walls have eyes."

★★★

Rob storms out of the mansion and stops dead in his tracks at the sight of Knucks, lying face down in the middle of the driveway with his wrists and ankles cuffed. Just as he is about to rush over and help up his cohort, Emmy leaps out from behind her S.U.V., gun drawn.

"Oh, damn, you're Lance's wife, right?" Rob asks with the detached, friendly tone of a checked-out employee.

"Get down on the ground," Emmy commands.

"What if I just left? Would that be cool? I won't call any backup, I promise."

Knucks lifts his head and glares at Rob. "What did you just say?"

"You heard me. I'm out. I'm tired of being everyone's bitch." Rob walks over to Knucks, pulls his keys from his pocket and looks at Emmy. "I won't call anyone. Trust me. It'd be just as dangerous for me as it would be for you."

Emmy stares into Rob's eyes. Finding no hint of deceit, she nods for him to leave.

"When I get out of these cuffs, I'm killing both of you," Knucks warns.

Rob laughs before calmly opening the driver's side door and hopping inside. After starting the engine, he rolls down his window and says to Emmy, "Tell Lance, I loved doing his play and I'm sorry I didn't put more effort into it. I wanted to, but killer over there would've never let me hear the end of it. Maybe someday, if we're still alive, Lance and I will work together again. He's a good dude."

Emmy nods with gratitude as Rob speeds down the driveway and into an uncertain future.

★★★

Duke gently picks up Art with both arms like a groom hoisting up his bride on their wedding day as Art protests, "Put me down, damn it!"

"Not a chance. At the rate you're movin', we're never gettin' outta here," Duke says as he jogs them down the dimly lit hotel hallway.

"If you tell a damn soul about this, I'll kill ya. I don't care if you saved my life."

Duke laughs. "I promise."

As they continue down the hall, Art points up ahead at the ceiling, "That's where that coward popped out and ambushed me."

Suddenly, a painting on the wall to their right with a chrome frame shoots out at them, hitting Duke in the head and sending both men crashing to the ground as Chet soars out from an opening in the wall, landing on Duke and immediately pummeling him with punches to the head. Amidst the fracas, Art manages to pull himself up and hurl his body at Chet, briefly knocking him off of Duke. As Duke attempts to grapple with his assailant, he quickly realizes that he is dealing with an equal in the realm of mixed martial arts. Reaching a stalemate, Chet glances to his right and sees Duke's pistol lying a few feet away. He quickly lunges for the gun, but Duke manages to swing his legs around and kick the gun down the hallway, out of Chet's reach.

As Chet breaks free from Duke's grasp, Art uses every ounce of energy left in him to stand up and delay Chet's attempt at the gun, but this time, Chet sees him coming and throws an expert haymaker squarely into Art's cheek, knocking him out cold. Just before Chet can pick up the gun, his legs go out from under him as Duke drops him to the floor, does a barrel roll, takes possession of the gun and points it at Chet.

"You move, I bust a cap," Duke warns as he catches his breath and blinks away the quickly building pain in his head. Keeping his gun aimed at a frozen Chet, he picks up Art and carries him toward the golden staircase.

From behind the desk in the hotel lobby below, Lars aims his hunting rifle at the top of the golden staircase. As soon as Duke comes into view, Lars fires a shot into Duke's thigh, sending both him and Art tumbling down the golden staircase while Chet sprints down the hall and grabs Duke's gun.

★★★

Inside the dark banquet hall, Lance continues to stare down, frozen in terror at the sight of an open, gold coffin with a ring of unlit torches surrounding it and the mummified remains of a man inside.

Suddenly, the sound of a rifle shot startles Lance out of his terror-induced stupor. Fearing the worst, he sprints in the direction of the noise and reaches a large double-doorway, slowly turning the knob and opening it just enough to glance into the lobby and see Willie Nelson holding a large rifle.

"This can't be real," Lance whispers to himself as he looks to the left and sees his wounded brother-in-law lying next to an unconscious Art with a tough-looking young man standing over them, pointing a pistol in their direction.

The terrifyingly surreal nature of the scene, combined with the revelation that this Willie Nelson impersonator with a penchant for cross-dressing whom he spent weeks directing is actually an evil genius, leaves Lance temporarily breathless. After regaining his composure and refilling his brain with oxygen, Lance begins to formulate a plan.

He pulls out his phone and snaps a picture of Willie through the crack in the door, then snaps a photo of his goon before pressing record on his voice memo app and hiding his phone in his pocket; his best attempt at wearing a wire.

With the easy part of the plan complete, Lance hesitates for a moment, makes an awkward sign of the cross, slowly opens both doors and declares with the air of a classic dramatist, "I am so sorry everyone! This whole thing is my fault."

Lars and Chet both stare at Lance in confused disbelief as he continues his address. "If I had just allowed Willie Nelson to be a woman, we could have avoided this whole calamity. You were set to give one of the greatest gender-bending performances in the history of theater and I stood in your path. It only makes sense that after such an indignation, you would engineer this reign of terror."

Lars points his rifle at Lance and replies with a mocking cackle, "You think I cared about that idiotic play? I only did that to create chaos."

Lance puts his hands up in surrender as he strikes a conciliatory note. "Listen, I understand your defensiveness. In the male-dominated corporate culture you grew up in, you never had the chance to properly express your feminine side."

"Are you going shoot this dude or what?" Chet asks, still confused at the references to his uncle playing a woman.

"Shut up, Chet," Lars barks back, weighing whether it would be better for his pride to verbally defend himself or put a bullet in Lance.

Lance turns to Chet, "I gotta say, in all my years in San Francisco, I never met a better drag queen than this man."

Lars' anger and embarrassment begins to rise as he shouts at Lance, "Shut up! Chet, call backup."

Before Chet can make his call, Lance interjects wistfully, "Willie, when you kissed Ronald during that rehearsal, it was like magic."

"You kissed Ronald?" Chet asks with the expression of a man who has just entered a soiled public bathroom.

Lance casts a lecturing eye on Chet and says, "Listen, Muscles, I will not stand here and allow you to judge this man for passionately kissing his stage-husband. He should be commended for his commitment."

"Alright, that's enough," Lars says as he aims his rifle and fires a shot at Lance, who manages to lunge to his left quickly enough to avoid the worst of the shot; the bullet just grazing his right shoulder. A painful flesh wound, no doubt, but not a fatal or maiming one.

★★★

A few minutes prior, when Emmy heard the first gunshot, she managed to keep her cool and stay outside, but now with the sound of a second gunshot, she no longer can contain herself or wait for the police. She takes a deep breath, pulls Knucks up from the ground and drags him to the front door, where she uses his fingerprint to unlock it just as Lars is about to follow Lance into the banquet hall and put a final bullet in him.

Lars stops in his tracks at the sound of the front door unlocking. He points his rifle at the entrance, which slowly opens to reveal a cuffed Knucks, held at gunpoint by Emmy who uses him as a human-shield.

"Drop the rifle!" Emmy shouts.

"You really think he's a good shield? After the way his crew has failed tonight? I'd almost rather kill him than you," Lars replies with an evil laugh before taking aim at Knucks, pulling the trigger and shooting him in the shoulder as Emmy jumps to her right, just in time to avoid getting hit by the exiting bullet.

As Emmy takes temporary refuge behind the small bar stand in the corner, evil Willie Nelson smiles with lustful glee and fires shot after shot at the bar, shattering bottles of alcohol and preventing Emmy from firing back at him. Just as he is about to reach the bar, Lance sprints from the banquet hall brandishing one of the torches from the coffin, now lit with a blazing flame. Chet attempts to fire a shot at Lance, but Duke reaches out, knocks the gun out of his hand and engages his adversary in another wrestling match as Lars spins around to see the flame of the torch hit him squarely in the face.

Despite his screaming pain and inability to see, Lars still manages to put up a fight as Lance attempts to wrestle the rifle free and tackle him to the ground. Emmy pops up from behind the bar and with stunning quickness, hits Lars with a knee to the head and assists Lance in pinning the madman to the ground.

Meanwhile, across the room, Chet quickly gains the upper hand on Duke, whose wounded leg leaves him ill-equipped for the fight. Behind them, a barely-conscious Art slowly pulls himself across the foot of the golden staircase, drops to one knee, picks up the pistol and laboriously aims it at Chet, who freezes as the sound of police sirens slowly becomes audible.

As the police sirens continue to grow louder, Ronald peeks his head into the house, takes stock of the carnage and says, "What'd I miss?"

An exasperated Emmy barks back at him, "What took you so long?"

"Well, initially, after realizing I didn't know the address of this place and would have to lead the police here and open the gate, which would then lead them to ask some uncomfortable questions that I was not prepared to answer, I decided I was going to just drive away and spend the rest of my life in hiding. But then I thought about all the people who would miss out on my gift if I were to disappear. To not be able to spend the rest of my life inhabiting the greatest characters on the biggest stages was just unthinkable. So, I decided to throw caution to the wind for the sake of my art, turn around, call the police and lead them here. And of course, I was concerned about you guys too..." Ronald says as he takes a closer look at the man that Emmy and Lance are holding down; his eyes nearly popping out of his head at the sight of Willie Nelson.

"Willie Nelson?! How did you get wrapped up in all this?"

"I'm the boss, you idiot. And you're a dead man," Lars replies through gritted teeth.

"Oh, man, I would love to shine a spotlight in your face right now. That would be such a perfect ending. When I write my screenplay about this, I'll include it."

Suddenly, a flood of police officers storm into the building and direct him to move out of the way, interrupting his train of thought and flipping him into actor-mode at the opportunity for a new audience. He adjusts his belt buckle like a masculine cowboy and addresses the officers with the tone of a confident lawman, "It's alright guys, I got it all under control. You're going to want to arrest burnt-faced Willie Nelson and the beefy guy over there... Oh, right, there are two beefy guys. Arrest the one who isn't bleeding."

Despite the fact that every officer is ignoring him, Ronald continues, "That looks bad by the way. Might want to call a bus for him; that's cop lingo for ambulance. Oh, should I start taking down their statements? I've seen every episode of *Blue Bloods,* so I know the drill..."

An exasperated Emmy looks over at Ronald and replies, "Ronald, please. Shut up."

Chapter Twenty-Six

Day 140 of Pregnancy

R onald carries an outlandishly large bouquet of flowers through the bustling lobby of the Baylor Health Center. Lance trails a few feet behind him, unenthusiastically holding a life-size teddy bear as Emmy walks beside him, arms awkwardly wrapped around a giant cardboard novelty check.

As they reach the elevators, Ronald presses the up button and the doors immediately open, revealing a space just large enough for the giant bouquet. "Should we have the bouquet air-lifted to the room or will it fit?" Lance quips, pressing the up button for a second elevator as Ronald squeezes into the first.

"I'll wait for you guys at the top," Ronald replies with a wink as the doors close.

"Whose idea was it to carpool again?" Emmy dryly asks.

"It was his," Lance answers with a sigh. "This is why I drive a compact car. You drive a monstrosity like yours and people will make you lug any number of items around for them."

Just before Emmy can fire back a retort, the sight of a bandaged, elderly man in a wheelchair reminds her of the purpose of their visit and casts a somber note upon the couple as they squeeze into the elevator.

A few moments later, the elevator doors open to reveal Ronald, already mid-conversation with two nurses, who laugh uproariously at the conclusion of his medical joke, which he read in his joke book the night before in preparation for the hospital visit. He glances to his left and sees his friends exit the elevator. "Sorry, I could spend all day talking to you ladies, but I have a hero to visit. Make sure you check out today's edition of the Dallas Morning News. Our play, *Purple Sky,* got a great review. That man walking down the hall with the giant teddy bear is actually kind of a celebrity. I'll get you our autographs on the way out."

Ronald blows a kiss to the nurses and rushes away in pursuit of Lance and Emmy, who reach Duke's hospital room and peek inside, finding him texting on his phone as Hank snores in the corner of the room and Lupita kneels beside him, deep in prayer.

"Who's this faker over here in the bed?" Emmy playfully asks.

"Sis!" Duke replies with genuine excitement as she leans the cardboard check against the wall and gives her brother a loving kiss on the cheek.

Lance stuffs the teddy bear into a nearby chair and gives Duke a long, unashamed hug. "Who knew my brother-in-law was Jason Bourne?"

"Get the in-law out of there. We're brothers," Duke corrects with an appreciative smile.

Lance offers a friendly nod and asks, "How'd the surgery go?"

"Perfect. Bullet is gone and the doc said within a year my leg should be good as new."

"Where should I put these?" Ronald asks, searching around the room for a flat surface large enough to hold the cartoonish bouquet.

"Those better be for my mom," Duke warns with machismo.

"You don't like them?" Ronald asks, genuinely surprised.

"They're beautiful, thank you, Ronald," Lupita interjects.

"I can return the stuffed animal…" Ronald offers.

"No, that thing is legit. I'm keepin' that," Duke says in complete seriousness. He looks over at the large check and asks, "What's with the novelty check?"

"That is from Art and Jack. Well, the cardboard was my idea, but as a token of gratitude for your heroism, Altitude Airlines is giving you two hundred thousand dollars to cover all your medical expenses, lost wages and maybe a down-payment on your own home," Ronald announces with pride. Duke stares in momentary shock then laughs out loud with gratitude and pulls Ronald in for a bear hug.

"How is Art?" Duke asks Emmy while still gripping Ronald in his powerful arms.

"He's doing well. Still recovering at home and annoyed that he can't work on his cars right now. But Jack and Maddie are taking good care of him and keeping watch. He refuses to talk to Ronald, but when Ronny here votes to install Jack as CEO, that should thaw things."

"Any word on Judith?" Duke asks.

Ronald suddenly grows emotional at the mentioning of his wife's name as Emmy calmly replies, "She's taking a plea deal and will get a reduced sentence for her co-operation, but it'll be at least a couple years until she's eligible for parole."

"What about that Willie Nelson creep? Will his lawyers get him off?"

"No, with the pictures and audio Lance gave the police, he's pretty well screwed on that front."

"Good," Duke replies with a chuckle. He turns to Ronald. "Are you and Judith goin' to split up?"

Ronald loudly blows his nose into a tissue and regains his composure. "Oh, yeah, it's over. I'm leaving her behind and going to Hollywooooooo! Although the whole conjugal visit thing does sound pretty enticing…"

"Alright, time to go. Sorry you had to hear that, Mom," Emmy says as she begins to usher Ronald out of the room.

"But I haven't read him our review yet! We're the toast of Dallas!" Ronald protests as he and Emmy exit.

Lance places his hand on Dukes shoulder and says, "Thank you for everything, my brother."

"Anytime, Yoga-Boy."

Just before Lance is about to leave, he turns to Lupita and looks deeply into her large, knowing eyes. "And thank you, Lupita. If you hadn't used your special powers, Duke never would have intervened in the first place."

"Not my powers… His," Lupita replies with a smile and a point to the Heavens as Hank continues to snore in the corner of the room.

Chapter Twenty-Seven

Day 271 of Pregnancy, Day 1 of Birth

Visions of fame and fortune fill his mind as Ronald drives south on Highway 101 with all of his remaining possessions in the bed of his pickup truck, ready for the next chapter of his life. He rounds a corner on the freeway and looks up in awe at Universal Studios Hollywood, perched high on the hill to his left as a nearby driver leans on his horn and flips him the bird.

"Even the road rage is cinematic!" Ronald says with genuine excitement as he smiles and waves at the angry man who cuts in front of him and speeds away.

After taking the Highland Ave exit, Ronald continues his drive like a wide-eyed child, rolling down the windows of his truck to take in all of the sounds and smells of his grungy wonderland. A few stoplights later, he waves at a middle-aged man walking on the sidewalk next to him and says, "Ted Danson?! Is that you?"

The pedestrian, who clearly is not Ted Danson, turns to Ronald and smiles, revealing a plethora of missing teeth.

"Yikes, Ted really has let himself go," Ronald says to himself as he continues his drive into Hollywood, scanning every sidewalk for more celebrities. Thinking Lance would love to enjoy some of the sights, Ronald pulls out his phone and puts in a video-call to Lance, but comes up empty.

"He's probably gettin' an earful from his new boss," Ronald says to himself as he places a voice-call to Lance. After a few rings and Lance's voice-mail greeting, Ronald says into the phone, "Superstar! It's your best friend. Just wanted to let you know I made it safely to Hollywood. I figure you're probably teaching one of your classes or getting yelled at by Principal Dwyer. I can't imagine working for that guy. But those kids are lucky. I wish I had a teacher like you when I was in High School. Anyway, I'll send you some pictures of famous people I hang out with. And keep me posted if there's any news on the baby-front! Could be any day now!"

After a grueling ten hours of labor, Emmy and Lance cry tears of joy as they look down at their newborn baby, Anthony. Every cry from Anthony is like music to their ears as the doctor informs them that their little boy is healthy and his vitals are strong.

Lance pulls out his phone to take a video of Emmy and Anthony, briefly glancing at and bypassing the notifications from Ronald, before capturing the sight of his son, pressed up against his wife's chest. The loss of San Francisco, the culture shock of Dallas, the homicidal maniacs, all fade into oblivion in this blessed moment of love. This new life bursting onto the scene, ready to send Emmy and Lance on the biggest adventure of their lives.

Epilogue

The vast Los Angeles skyline glistens below a purple evening sky as Ronald rests his elbows on an upper story ledge of the Griffith Observatory and stares with wonder, occasionally turning to hand his business card to people he hopes are entertainment executives, but really are just confused tourists.

After being kicked out of a planetarium show for loudly and repeatedly cracking jokes, Ronald grumpily returns to his truck. Just before hopping in, he sees a note wedged under his left windshield wiper and removes it. He looks around the parking lot for signs, assuming it is yet another parking ticket, but a rush of fear courses through his body as he looks down at the note that reads: "YOU ARE NOT WELCOME HERE. GO BACK TO DALLAS, OR DIE. SINCERELY, THE NETWORK

Acknowledgments

First and foremost, I'd like to thank my wife, Tina, without whom this book would not have been possible. Her contributions to my life and my work are immeasurable; including the sweet little man she carried in her womb for nine months and gave birth to (Emmy's pregnancy struggles were just the tip of the iceberg of what Tina endured!).

Thank you to my incredible parents, Dennis and Valerie, whose constant love, support and honest feedback are the foundation upon which my entire life and career have been built. It would take a War and Peace-length memoir to fully capture the breadth of their selflessness and grace through the many storms our family endured.

By the same token, big shout out to my ride-or-die siblings, Justin and Mollie, for their contributions to this book and for always looking out for me, loving me, and cheering me on. And to Mollie's brilliant husband, Cesar, whose deeply faithful, Peruvian-Texan mother, Mimi, provided considerable inspiration for Lupita.

Deep thanks to my Aunt Sharon, Uncle Norman and Uncle Erwin, who exposed me to San Francisco's vast array of artistic, performative and cultural experiences from the moment I could sit up straight and who always make sure no matter where I roam, the city by the bay still feels like home.

Although Lance is not based on any one person and our in-laws are different, he and I are both high maintenance in our own ways and I want to thank my wife's family for welcoming this idiosyncratic comedian into their family.

Thank you to my stellar manager, Christine King, whose invaluable notes and encouragement were so helpful during this process.

I am beyond grateful to my graphic designer/illustrator extraordinaire, Conor McCammon, who made my cover dreams come true, and once again, made me look way cooler than I actually am. And thank you to my fabulous photographer, Janaye Culton for teaching me the true meaning of the word "smize."

Many thanks to my *David's Ark* crew, Luke Lacoy and James Creviston, for their support of this project, wonderful feedback, and overall awesomeness.

And finally, I'm thankful to the joyful, loving version of the Catholic faith that I encountered in the midst of the darkest period of my life. I have been both an insider and an outsider of the church and I have a deep appreciation for the struggle that everyone goes through to find their unique place in this world.

I hope that *Lone Star Lance* brought you, dear reader, some joy and a respite from whatever stresses you may be dealing with in the craziness of life.

About the Author

David Studebaker is a stand-up comedian, writer, actor filmmaker, and host. He has been featured on a variety of television shows and his stand-up can be heard on Sirius XM Radio. David was the host of *Pivot On The Street* for Pivot TV's National Network, has emceed multiple awards shows, including the Last Chance for Animals Celebrity Awards Gala at the Beverly Hilton and won "Best Director" at the Oregon Documentary Film Festival for his hit docu-series: *David's Ark*. In April of 2019 he took on the biggest project of his life: the birth of his first-born son, who has provided a wealth of material and poopy diapers. Originally from the San Francisco Bay Area, he now resides in Los Angeles with his wife, Tina, his two dogs, and Matthew, the aforementioned poop-dispenser.

Made in the USA
Columbia, SC
29 October 2020